MIRACLE AT HOLLY HILL INN

MADDIE JAMES

MIRACLE AT HOLLY HILL INN

A Dickens Holiday Romance

Maddie James

Sign up here for news of contests, giveaways, and new releases.
https://www.maddiejames.net/p/newsletter.html

MIRACLE AT HOLLY HILL INN

Sometimes all we need is to believe.

Ariana Angelo's blog specializes in "all things Christmas, all year long." While traveling New England in search of the perfect Christmas village, she lands in Dickens amid the town's Christmas festivities—and a snowstorm. She's delighted and giddy with holiday cheer and can literally feel the magic of the season in her bones.

Matt Matthews—owner of the century-old Dickens Hardware—despite all the Christmastime holiday hoopla, dislikes the season. He's all about regular business—not a holiday ornament or tree trimming bauble to be found in his store. The holiday triggers unwanted memories, so he avoids the festivities—and the people—as much as possible.

While she set out to find the perfect Christmas village, Ariana instead finds the town Scrooge. Will two days snowbound together at the historic Holly Hill Inn bring them closer together on their holiday differences, or send them each on their merry way?

ONE

D*ecember 22, Present Day*

EVEN THE TREES SPARKLE.

Ariana Angelo pushed open her car door and stepped out onto the snow-covered pavement. In awe, she scanned her surroundings to take in the quaint New England Main Street lined with Victorian shopfronts—each one decorated to storybook perfection with greenery and red bows, a hefty portion of tinsel and holly, and of course, snow.

The snow was real. None of that fake stuff like back home.

Closing the car door, she moved toward the sidewalk, twirling once, maybe twice, still perusing the most precious Christmas village scene she'd ever before encountered—and that was saying a lot. Christmas was her business, her world—and this town just might be Christmas perfection. She was so glad she'd come.

Stifling the urge to lift her face to the sky and catch a

drifting fluffy snowflake on her tongue, she sighed with happiness, eager to explore.

Down the street sat the gazebo. She recognized it from pictures she'd seen of the town. It, too, was draped in greenery and ribbons, looking somewhat like a confection sitting atop some sort of pretty Christmas cake—at least one she might bake. It appeared the gazebo was situated within the town square. Beside it was a statue sporting a red scarf billowing in the brisk breeze. Stepping onto the snow-swept sidewalk, she kept an eye on the structure and wandered a few steps in that direction.

There.

Off to the side of the gazebo stood the town square Christmas tree, proudly displaying gold and silver baubles, ornaments of all colors, and more ribbons—all peeking through fresh snow. The annual Dickens Christmas tree lighting was earlier in the season, and she was sorry she'd missed it—but there was no denying the tree's magnificence.

And, oh? Is that a carousel?

Her insides twittered with glee, bubbling up so rapidly she could barely contain it. She might have let out a quick little giggle.

Pausing her stroll, she spied a colorful sign hanging in the shop window to her right. Her eye traveled over the shopfront —Leslie's Bakes & More—and her tummy rumbled. Another cup of coffee soon, and perhaps a pastry, would be nice.

Her gaze landed on the red and green sign. *Holiday Lighting Event at Holly Hill Inn, Thursday Evening, December 23rd.* With a quick look at the calendar on her digital watch, she smiled. Yes. Today was Wednesday, so the lighting event at the inn was tomorrow—on the eve of Christmas Eve, or Christmas Eve Eve, as she liked to say. Why not stretch out the holiday as long as possible?

Smiling, and immensely happy she'd braved the snowstorm —even against her family's warnings—she felt silly with holiday cheer. The weather had been dicey the day before, delaying her trip into historic Dickens. While she didn't mind getting stuck an extra night at the small New England B&B she'd booked about sixty miles down the road, she was glad the storm had let up enough so she could get to Dickens.

And *bonus!* Because of a cancelation and a matter of happenstance, she had secured a reservation for three nights at the popular Holly Hill Inn, although she was in no hurry to get there. Too much to explore first in the village. Besides, she couldn't check in until late afternoon—so she had most of the daylight hours left to discover the magic of Dickens at Christmastime.

Dickens just might be the small-town Christmas village of her dreams. She couldn't wait to get pictures and write about it. Her blog readers were going to be so excited.

Reaching into her bag, she pulled out her camera, adjusted the lens, and began walking. As if by magic, the town suddenly teemed with shoppers, milling in and out of the shops, chatting on the sidewalks, and calling out holiday greetings.

Shopping for last-minute gifts before this storm hits again, she guessed.

Ariana smiled, dizzy with Christmas excitement and filled with the holiday spirit. She snapped pictures, chatted with the townsfolk, and gleefully made her way up Main Street, around the square, and down the other side.

Her heart was happy.

It was Christmas and she was finally in Dickens.

Nothing could spoil her mood. Absolutely nothing.

MATT MATHEWS PULLED the bottom of his sweater sleeve over the heel of his palm and rubbed out the smudges his breath made on the old windowpane. Peering out into the street —perusing the local shoppers and visiting tourists—he sighed. His breath, once again, fogged the glass, so he took one more swipe at it and then turned away.

How many more days until Christmas was over? Too many.

Heading back to his cubby-hole refuge behind the old wooden countertop desk, tucked into the back of the hardware store, he traveled the center aisle between time-worn, nearly ceiling-high, wooden shelves which housed everything from plumbing and electrical supplies to household cleaners and associated paraphernalia, some small appliances like electric can openers and hand-held mixers, and tools. Lots of tools.

And where there were tools, there were also items that went along with tools—like fence wire, and tape measures, and replacement doorknobs, and cabinet pulls, and such.

Instead of shelves in those areas, there were small wooden drawers—carefully catalogued by his Great Uncle Herb years ago—where one could select nails or screws or bolts or washers, or an assortment of those and other items that a carpenter, or perhaps a crafty person might need.

Yes. Dickens Hardware held all that and more. His family had always strived to provide the town with what they needed, so variety was the mainstay.

What one wouldn't find at Dickens Hardware, however—a store that had been in his family for over a hundred years—was anything to do with Christmas. No tinsel. No trees. No ornaments, holly, wrapping paper, wreaths, or mistletoe.

Ever.

Well, that wasn't entirely true. His parents had stocked quite a bit of holiday cheer and such in the past. They loved the holiday. But Matt? No. He'd done away with all that years ago.

Christmas was not his thing. It was not his busy season. People weren't shopping for hammers or toilet plungers in December. They were out for holly and wreaths. And truth be known, he'd probably be better off next year to close the store the entire month of December and go someplace warm for a while—some place where the entire town didn't revel in the idea of the holiday or focus eleven months of the year getting ready for it.

Yes. That is a good idea. Some place warm.

Matt settled himself on the stool behind the counter, crossed his arms over his chest, and peered out over the store. At some point soon, he should think about walking down the street to grab some lunch—but did he really want to brave the crowd?

Maybe he'd just close the store early and go home. He could always open a can of soup. "Merry Christmas to me."

ARIANA IMPATIENTLY PEEKED around the line in front of her at Leslie's Bakes & More, trying to get a glimpse at the counter to see what kind of cookies were hiding in front of a gentleman standing there waiting for his sandwich. She tapped her foot, inspecting the quaint interior of the business. Patience was not her strong suit, so waiting in line for anything was always a challenge. In the meantime, she'd simply busy herself by perusing the Christmas decorations and the people, the confections and pastries, and the deli menu in the small bakery-slash-sandwich shop.

Which was not a bad idea, she surmised, to combine the two types of establishments. The bakery could cater to the breakfast crowd with pastries and coffee earlier in the day, then later, sandwiches and cookies for the lunch crowd. And pie.

Oh, there was pie. She stretched her neck and took a tiny step to her right to ogle the pie case around the corner from the counter.

Leaning more to her right, she watched the gentleman hiding the cookies step away—*were those Snickerdoodles?*—and the line moved forward.

She took a half-step to the right, then another—but someone darted in front of her, taking her spot in line.

Standing there for a moment, a little befuddled to be perfectly honest, she made the best of it.

"Excuse me." She tapped the man's shoulder. "I'm sure you didn't realize you cut in front of me. I've been standing here for a while. But if you are in a hurry, I'm happy to let you go first. Besides, it's Christmas." She smiled.

He turned and looked at her, mumbled something under his breath, and didn't smile back. "You weren't in line."

"Oh, but I was. Am." Her feet planted, she peered back, not about to move.

He stared back at her with his knit cap pulled down low over his forehead, a shock of brown hair poking out, and his arms crossed tightly over his coat at his chest. "I, also, have been standing in line. You, it appeared, had stepped away and were gawking."

Gawking? "I beg your pardon?"

"Gawking," he replied. "You know, gallerwaggling about. Listlessly wandering. You didn't appear to be standing in line. I thought you were, basically, aimlessly perusing."

Ariana squinted, quickly studying the man. He wasn't an old man. He was, perhaps, a couple of years older than her—but his grumpiness gave off an illusion of being much older—and crotchety. Such a shame. He actually had pleasant features —high cheekbones, a firm chin, and a scruffy five o'clock shadow that was maybe two days overdue.

She stood a little straighter and set her shoulders. *Forget about the sexy five o'clock shadow, Ariana.* "For the record, I do not gallerwag. Nor do I listlessly wander or aimlessly peruse. I'll have you know that should I ever peruse or wander, I do so with intent. And as to gallerwag? You made that up. It's not a word. Perhaps you meant lollygag."

"No. I meant what I said. Look it up." He turned into the line, showing her his back.

Not to be dismissed, Ariana poked him on the shoulder again with her forefinger. "I actually don't carry a dictionary with me. Besides, words are my business and that is not one."

He shrugged. "Got your phone? Google it." He gave her a backward glance.

"I most certainly will." Reaching for her purse and her phone, she paused, then looked at the back of his head. "Later. You are intentionally distracting me."

He half-turned. "You were already distracted."

Sidling up next to him, she made eye contact. Just for the record, she noted to herself, they were deep brown and...well, right now, they were sort of probing hers. "I'll have you know I was not distracted. I'm an observer. A writer. I examine things. You came from nowhere and simply cut in line in front of me."

"Not exactly correct." He took a step forward with the moving line. "I've been standing behind you for a few minutes. You stepped out of line, so...."

"I most certainly did not step out of line." She countered his step and took another one ahead of him.

"Are you cutting in front of me?"

"Just reclaiming my place in line."

"Oh, no. I'm next."

In exasperation, Ariana clenched her fists and glared at him. "My God. What a Scrooge." She thought she heard

7

someone off to the side snicker. Glancing that way, she realized they'd become the center of attention.

Great.

He made direct eye contact again with her, leaned in a bit, and then said loudly and clearly, "Bah. Humbug."

"Next." The young man behind the counter called out.

Swiftly turning, Ariana blurted, "Medium black coffee and three of those cookies." She pointed to the Snickerdoodles.

"The usual, Tom," the man said simultaneously.

Tom eyed them both.

Ariana refused to look at the man standing next to her. *The usual?* A local. Suddenly, her impression of the town was slightly soured, but she would not let that sway her.

"Coming right up," Tom said. He turned to the man. "Matt, please try not to run off the paying customers."

"Far be it from me..." the man called Matt said.

She stared at him. He looked down at her.

Ariana broke eye contact and looked ahead, waiting for her coffee and cookies. After several long seconds of drumming her fingertips on the counter, she sighed when he set a cup of coffee and a white bag of cookies in front of her.

"Four dollars and ninety-eight cents, ma'am."

She opened her wallet.

"Put it on mine, Tom," the man next to her said.

Immediately, she protested. "Oh, no. I'll get it. But thank you."

"My pleasure." He nodded to Tom.

"I mean, I'll take care of my bill."

He peered down. "Welcome to Dickens. I hope you enjoyed your stay. Be careful on your way out of town."

Ariana gathered her coffee and cookies, then looked back up at the guy. "Well, thank you, but I'm not leaving. In fact, I just got here and am planning to stay for a few days. I appreciate the warm welcome." The saccharin sweet smile she tossed him almost made her nauseous. But no matter, she decided right then and there, she would not let this single, unhappy incident spoil her mood—or her impression of Dickens.

"Merry Christmas," she said, turning to leave.

He grunted something.

Ariana paused, her gaze straight ahead, and headed out of the shop.

TWO

A s she stepped out onto the sidewalk, Ariana abruptly stopped. Townspeople and tourists scurried off to their vehicles or into buildings, obviously sent scattering by the blustery gust of wind zipping down Main Street. Snow swirled furiously and fell at a rapidly increasing pace. Firmly grasping her bag of cookies and her coffee, pulling them closer to her chest, Ariana put her head down against the snow and wind and headed to her car parked a few spaces away.

With a click of her key fob, her rental car door unlocked. She slipped inside, and the door shut tight.

"Whew. That came up quick."

She sat for a moment, placed the coffee in the cupholder, and removed her gloves. The smell of cinnamon and sugar tickled her nose as she opened the white bag. *Ah, a little bit of heaven....*

Her shoulders relaxed as she reached for a cookie. About to take a bite, she looked out her windshield—which was quickly piling up with heavy, cold wet stuff—and watched the gentleman from inside the coffee shop eyeball her sitting in her car as he passed. She made eye contact, just as she was popping a Snickerdoodle into her mouth, and he glanced away. Following him, she watched as he scurried along, his head down, while passing five shops and then turning left, and finally entering a store on the corner. Her gaze traveled up to read the sign over the shop: *Dickens Hardware.*

"Bah humbug to you," she said aloud, and rolled her eyes.

But her gaze stayed on the shop, and she examined it for a moment. Something was...different from the other shops. Odd that she hadn't even noticed before, but the shop practically disappeared into the scene and didn't stand out at all.

Oh. She glanced up and down the street. "Well, that's ridiculous. It's the only shop not decorated for Christmas."

Bah Humbug. The man's words echoed in her brain.

"I believe we have a modern-day Scrooge on our hands here." She pondered that for a moment, watching the shop front—then shrugging, she popped the last bite of cookie in her mouth. "And none of my business."

Pushing the unwelcome experience aside, she grappled in her bag for her phone. After tapping in the Holly Hill Inn address on her GPS map app, she backed the car out and followed the directions. She was still a little early to check in, but with the snow kicking up, it was probably best she got there soon. The inn was located a few miles out of town. Hopefully, the owner wouldn't mind if she waited inside.

It took all of twenty-one minutes to find the inn.

Tucked back off the road at the end of Holly Hill Lane, the inn finally came into view. Ariana could barely see it through the snow squall until she got closer—a splash of red popped through the blowing white, guiding her like a beacon. She maneuvered the circular drive and parked, eyeing the old inn with delight. What she could see of the home sent the giddy in her tummy soaring right up to her heart—red painted

11

clapboards with white trim and a picket fence bordering the front of the property, all dripped with greenery, red bows, and twinkling white lights. There were candles in the windows on the porch. A brick walk—which appeared recently swept but drifting over again—was framed at the entrance by a wide lattice-work arch. The brick rambled through a garden area, one that was likely enchanting in the spring, lead to the front portico of the old home.

And there were holly bushes, right and left, lining the brick sidewalk.

Ariana reluctantly left her car, cookies tucked into her purse, coffee in hand, and camera bag over her shoulder. With her head lowered against the blowing snow, she made her way to the trunk of her car and retrieved her rolling bag. It took a few minutes to lug it all up to the porch—the wheels on the luggage kept icing up—finally, she just carried it the rest of the way. Out of the snow and standing in front of a beautiful wooden front door, she shook herself and stomped her feet to remove as much snow as possible, brushed snow and hair out of her face, and headed for the doorbell.

A woman opened the door before she got there, drawing her sweater about her, and stepping out onto the porch. "Ariana Angelo?"

"Yes. I'm early. I hope you don't mind."

"Oh no." Smiling warmly, the woman reached for Ariana's luggage. "It's not a problem. Please, come in."

They shuffled inside. The innkeeper led the way and Ariana followed. She noticed the woman tap the Holly Hill Inn sign to the right of the door as she entered and wondered what that was all about.

"Let me take your coffee," she said, turning back to Ariana. She grasped the paper cup and set it aside. "There's more coffee in the kitchen, or hot cocoa if you like. But let's get you out of these wet things first."

Nodding, Ariana set her purse on a nearby bench. "Anything hot would be lovely. Thank you."

"Of course." The woman smiled. "You can leave your boots here." She pointed to a large welcome mat by the door, where a few pairs of shoes and boots lined the entry. Then she helped Ariana out of her coat, hanging in on a hall tree by the door. "I'll roll your bag over to the desk and meet you there."

Kicking out of her boots, Ariana placed them on the mat, then turned to peruse the entryway to the inn.

She sighed. *I'm finally here.*

Christmas. Everywhere, there was Christmas. Holly, tinsel, twinkling lights, ornaments, and more lit up the festive entryway. And the spicy aroma wafting down the hallway smelled heavenly. Christmas cookies? Fruitcake? Her heart danced.

A lovely fir tree stood in the corner, decorated with what looked to be handmade decorations. Ariana drifted to it and as she touched and explored the ornaments, felt a strong sense of family. "These are beautiful," she whispered.

"Yes. Three generations of ornaments, all decorated by children," the woman said, and then stepped around the counter closer to Ariana. She put out her hand. "Hi. I'm Kat Hall, by the way, owner of Holly Hill Inn. We spoke on the phone. I should have said that earlier."

Ariana shook her hand and smiled. "I assumed. I'm thrilled to meet you. This tree is simply stunning. Do you mind if I take pictures?"

Kat shook her head. "Not at all. If I remember correctly, you're a writer—a blogger—and a photographer. Right?"

"Yes. Blogging mostly, but I'm trying to get into magazine work, too. For the writing, that is. My photography skills are fine for the blog but not for a slick magazine. Christmas is my niche." She glanced back at the tree. "And, I should say I'll need your written permission for photographs. I have a sample release we can look at later if that's okay with you."

"Sure." Kat grinned. "I figure it's all advertising, right? I've no problem with pictures."

Ariana thought about getting her camera out and taking a picture of the tree and ornaments right then, but thought better of it. She had plenty of time. She fingered a tree decoration—a wooden cut-out of a nutcracker soldier—rather imperfectly painted.

"My brother painted that one," Kat said. "I think he was ten."

"I love that it's sort of messy. Sort of primitive."

"It lends a bit of charm, doesn't it?"

Ariana noticed Kat staring at the ornament. She shook herself and looked away. "Let's get you checked in. Your room is ready. I hoped you would get here early. I think we're in for a pretty significant snowfall tonight."

"Oh? More?"

"Oh, yes."

"This last gust came up fast."

Kat looked up. "Well, according to the weather people, it may stall over us. Who knows how much snow we will get? The storm pushed through quickly from the west, but some sort of pressure out over the coast might hold it here in the valley for a while. I guess we'll get what we'll get." She studied her. "How do you feel about being snowbound?"

"Seriously?"

Shrugging, Kat went back to writing something on a card. "Who knows?"

A smile bubbled up inside her and burst across her lips—she could feel it—and Ariana had to contain her giggle. "You know, Kat? I almost can't think of anything else I would love more than to be snowbound at Christmas in a lovely place like this."

Kat glanced up, reached for Ariana's hand, and beamed. "What a sweet thing to say. And refreshing. Usually when people get stranded here, they are cranky."

Laughing, Ariana returned, "I assure you I will not be cranky."

"You're a woman after my heart."

"I love Christmas."

Just then, the front door burst open, and Ariana turned toward the commotion.

"Mommy!" A little girl shouted while tumbling inside, slamming the door, dropping a backpack with a thud, and shrugging out of her coat—which landed in a heap in front of the door—while also kicking out of her boots. "We got out of Christmas Camp early. The bus brought me. The big snow is coming!"

The child rushed forward while Kat rounded the desk. "Aimee Hall." She halted the child with a look and crossed arms. "Where are your manners? Please say hello to Miss Angelo, our guest."

The little girl halted, sighed, and looked at Ariana. "Hello. Sorry. I'm Aimee." She stuck out her hand, much like her mother had done earlier.

Ariana crouched and took the child's small hand in hers and shook it. "I'm Ariana. Nice to meet you. How old are you?"

"I'm six." The little girl beamed, obviously proud of herself.

Smiling, Ariana said, "I thought as much. I have a six-year-old niece. Wow, your hands are like ice!" She rubbed the girl's hands between her own.

Aimee looked up at her mother. "Lost them again."

Kat rolled her eyes. "I'll find you another pair of mittens.

Now, go back and hang up that coat, put your boots on the mat, and take your backpack up to your room. The Camp called, so I knew you were coming. Cookie ingredients are waiting in the kitchen, and we have work to do. Now, go on, and don't forget to wash those hands."

Aimee grinned, displaying two missing front teeth. "Awesome. I love baking cookies. Will you bake with us, Miss Angelo?"

Taken aback a little, Ariana glanced at Kat. "Well, I... I don't want to impose. This sounds like a mother-daughter moment."

Kat laughed. "Oh please. I get a lot of those around here. We could use your help if you want to bake. I always appreciate another set of hands. But only if you want to."

"Please?" Aimee jumped up and down, grinning.

With a tip of her chin, Ariana said, "Only if you call me Ariana."

Aimee stuck out her hand again. "Deal!"

"Deal." Ariana hesitated no longer and shook Aimee's hand. "I'd love to."

Kat's fists settled on her hips. "Well then. Let's get you both upstairs. We will meet in the kitchen in fifteen minutes. All right, ladies?"

"All right, Mommy." Aimee bounded toward the stairwell.

Ariana retrieved her purse from the bench.

Kat turned back to the desk. "I just need your signature on this card, Ariana, and then I'll grab your key and we will get you to your room." She pushed the card across the desk, along with a pen.

Ariana took the pen and started to sign.

"Just note that I left the end date open—who knows when you'll be leaving here."

Jerking her head up, Ariana caught Kat's gaze. "You're serious about the snow, aren't you?"

Kat's eyes twinkled as she grinned back. "Anything is possible in Dickens at Christmas, and for some quirky reason, I have a feeling you will be here for a long time."

"Oh, really?" Ariana pushed the card across the counter.

Kat winked and turned toward the stairs.

"WHAT IS your favorite kind of cookie, Aimee?"

Shifting around Kat to grab a cooling rack from underneath the kitchen island, Ariana sidestepped Aimee and placed it on the countertop. Bending to peek into the oven window, she inspected the sugar cookies, waiting for just the right second to take them out. She had a theory—you take them out when they are slightly golden on top, and they will come out chewy in the middle and crispy around the edges, just how she liked them.

"I love Pecan Meltaways." Aimee crouched to look in the oven window too. "But those sugar cookies look so good, I can't wait to get the icing on them."

Smiling, Ariana rose and headed back to the island. "Me too. They will have to cool for a while first, but let's get started on making the icing."

"I know," Aimee singsonged. "Mommy says it too. Ice them too quickly and the good stuff melts right off."

"Exactly." Scooting around Kat again, who was busy layering the ingredients for chocolate toffee bars, Ariana rummaged in a utensil drawer for a rubber spatula when she spied a bamboo skewer and picked it up. "Oh, that's perfect."

She headed back to the oven.

"You sure know your way around a kitchen," Kat told her.

Crouching again, watching for the golden tint to pop up on

the cookies, Ariana sighed. "Well, my mom is a baker. She's been big on Christmas baking since I can remember. We still bake every year. Except, well, I'm not with her this year."

"Oh?" Kat wiped her hands on a kitchen towel. "Why not?"

Ariana popped her head up and smirked. "Because I'm here."

Laughing, Kat pointed. "Of course. What are you doing with that skewer?"

"This." Standing, Ariana pulled open the oven door, stepped back for a second as the heat escaped, then carefully poked a skewer into one cookie in the middle of the pan, quickly removed it, and brought it closer to inspect it. "Perfect."

"Clean?"

"Yes. And it's long enough to get to a middle cookie so you don't burn yourself."

"Wonderful tip."

Ariana grabbed an oven mitt. "Yes, and I never worry about the big hole in the middle because that's the one I'll eat first! They need to be taste-tested, right?"

Kat laughed. "Even more brilliant."

Smiling to herself, Ariana reached into the oven. "Let's get these out to cool."

A phone rang from somewhere. Kat glanced toward the kitchen door. "Drat, that's mine. It's on the desk in the entry. Aimee, can you run for it?"

"Got it, Mommy."

"Thanks, sweetie."

Ariana studied Kat, then perused the kitchen. Reaching for the camera she'd set off to the side, she snapped a few quick pictures of Kat working, and of the trays of cookies scattered about the kitchen. After a minute, she stashed her camera back in a cabinet, safe from the cookie makings.

Returning her attention to the sugar cookies, she said, "We've done some serious work here. These need to cool for a minute before putting them on the racks. I'll get started on the frosting." She measured some powdered sugar into a bowl.

"And we've lots more to do, I'm afraid." Kat lifted a spatula and slid it under a cookie. "With the lighting event here tomorrow evening, I like to have plenty of goodies on hand. Who knows how many people will show up?" She shrugged, touching a cookie top. "I think these are cool enough to move now."

"Great."

"Mommy?" Aimee called out. "Uncle Matt is on the phone."

"What does he want?"

Ariana could hear Aimee talking to someone in the other room. Did she say Uncle *Matt*? Second time today she'd heard that name. She shrugged that off, watching Kat finish up the candy layer on the toffee bars, then retrieved the milk from the refrigerator.

"Says he needs his room tonight. Okay?"

Ariana caught Kat's eye as she stopped what she was doing and glanced her way. Her lower lip curled into her mouth and she bit it. Suddenly, Kat appeared a bit perplexed.

"Everything okay?"

"That's my brother," she said.

"Oh."

"I guess if he needs to stay here tonight, the roads must be closed heading out to his farm. Lord knows you wouldn't catch him here at Christmastime for any other reason."

"Oh." Ariana looked to the kitchen door where Aimee had just appeared.

"Well?" Aimee asked, tapping her toe on the plank floor.

"Of course." Kat told her. "We only have one guest tonight

19

and it's Ariana. His room is clean and ready. Tell him dinner is at six if he wants to eat with us."

"Okay." Aimee ran off with the phone again, chattering with her uncle.

Ariana put a tablespoon of milk into the sugar bowl, added a bit of vanilla, and whisked. She thought about what Kat had just said. "So, if the roads are closed, then probably the businesses in town are closed, too. Right? And the restaurants?"

Nodding, Kat said, "Likely so."

"I see..." She picked up a bottle of red food coloring and tipped it to add two drops to the sugar mix. "I was hoping this would blow over so I could explore the town this evening and maybe grab dinner there." She stirred the color with a wooden spoon.

Kat sidled a look her way. "Where did you say you were from?"

"California."

"Ah. You don't know much about snow. Do you?"

"Well, not really."

Kat faced her, smiling. "Snow just doesn't blow over around here. It whips around and stays with us for days on end sometimes."

"Oh. So, no restaurants or shopping?"

"Probably not happening in your near future, Ariana, sorry to say. Besides, you're having dinner with us."

"Oh no. This is a bed-and-breakfast, not a bed-and-dinner."

Kat laughed and pulled out some plastic wrap to cover the toffee bars. "Not when you're snowbound. We feed whoever lands on our doorstep."

She guessed that made sense. "I'll pay you, of course."

Kat turned back with a stern look. "You most certainly will not. Besides, you are working your tail off here this afternoon. I think you've earned your supper."

"Well, if you are sure."

"I wouldn't have it any other way," Kat said. "Oh, and that frosting you've been stirring is getting a little hard. Think it needs to go on the cookies?"

Ariana, realizing she'd gotten a bit distracted, laughed. "Right. I'm on it."

MATT STOMPED the snow off his boots, twisted the knob on the heavy front door to the inn, and stepped inside. The house was warm and, as always this time of the year, practically glowing. As much as he despised the season, his sister loved it.

If the road to his farm hadn't been closed, he wouldn't even be here....

No use pondering that. The situation was what it was.

His boots on the mat and his coat on a hook, he ambled in sock feet down the hallway toward the kitchen of the old home. He'd grown up here, so he knew the way by heart. He'd not been here often, though, in recent years, keeping mostly to himself.

His sister inherited the place after their parents died. She'd been too young then to take it over, but the property was held in trust until she turned a legal age. Same thing happened for him with the hardware store. His father's attorney managed the estates until it was time, then it was up to each of them.

Laughter bubbled down the hallway from the kitchen and when he stepped inside the door, his heart sank. Kat mentioned dinner at six, but with the looks of the kitchen, he doubted that was happening soon. Boxes of decorated cookies, remnants of sugar and frosting, and sparkling decorations were scattered everywhere. Christmas music played from Kat's phone, propped up against a flour cannister. Not a nook or cranny was without a container or two of tasty confections.

The room oozed of Christmas, attitude and all.

"Whoa. What is all this?"

Kat swiveled from where she was talking with someone—a guest, probably—and looked at him. "Hey, Matt. These are for the lighting tomorrow."

"And you think that is still going to happen with this snow?"

She rolled her eyes. "First, as you know, I'm an optimist. Second, it's happening whether there are four people or a hundred. It's tradition, as you know."

"Bah. I doubt you will get four people."

"You don't have to be so negative."

Aimee giggled. "Oh, Uncle Matt. You are so silly. See? We have four people now. One. Two. Three. Four." She pointed to him, her mother, herself, and the guest.

Matt looked at the woman. Her back was to him, but she slowly turned. She was wearing one of his mother's Christmas aprons, which immediately set him on edge. Dusted with flour or powdered sugar or something, she also had a stripe of blue icing on her cheek—which, if he would admit it, looked kind of cute on her. He was certain her shoulder-length blond hair didn't normally sport a streak of green sprinkles—*also cute*—although today, who knew for sure.

But it was the rolling pin she held in her hand like a weapon that wasn't so charming. Plus, she was staring hard at him, and—

"You," she said.

"No, it's you," he countered.

Kat looked from one to the other. "You two know each other?"

He eyed the woman. "We've met. If you could call it that."

Then, changing the subject and dismissing her, he glanced at his sister. "Did you say something about dinner?"

Kat looked none too pleased. He would be happy to leave the subject and the festivities in the kitchen alone and find something to eat.

"There's beef and noodles in a slow-cooker on the buffet, along with rolls and a salad. Help yourself. We'll be along as soon as we wrap up here."

He glanced again to the woman. What was it about her that pleasantly irritated him?

Abruptly, she stuck out her hand. "I'm Ariana, by the way. We've not been properly introduced."

He stared at her hand, sugar and dough and all, but didn't take it. "Just call me Scrooge." He headed for the dining room.

"I think I already did."

A guffaw burst from his sister's lips, which annoyed him.

He shot her a "that's not funny" look and stopped in his tracks.

Spinning back, he ran his gaze over the three females, then landed on...what did she say her name was? *Ariana?* "And your point is?"

She shrugged. "No point. I just already had you pegged."

"For?"

"A Scrooge."

He held her gaze hostage for a moment. "And what makes you the expert?"

Ariana tipped her head to the side. "Well, to be perfectly honest, I am an expert on Christmas. And you possess all the qualities of a town Scrooge. Doesn't take one long to figure that out. You're grumpy. You don't even decorate your store for the holiday."

Kat looked at her. "Well, you are observant."

Dismissing his sister, he eyed the guest, this *Ariana*. Who in the heck was this pipsqueak of a woman who was hellbent on interrupting his regularly scheduled life? "A lot of details for a woman who hasn't even been in town for a day."

"Like I said, doesn't take long. Besides, I'm a—"

"Writer. I know. You're into details."

"Exactly."

"So, pat yourself on the back, *Little Miss Christmas*. You got it right. I am a Scrooge, and don't you forget it." He turned toward the dining room and the beef and noodles. A thought struck him, and he twisted back. "And don't you go getting any ideas about reforming me. Got it?"

The woman saluted. "Yes, sir."

Suddenly, he was famished. "Are you finished?"

"Probably not."

He stopped at the door. "What the hell does that mean?"

"Matt, watch your language."

He threw Kat a look. "Sorry." Pivoting back, he caught Ariana's gaze again. "Look. I am what I am. You are what you are. We'll never get together on this thing, so let's not try. Got it? Now, I'm tired and hungry, and if you all don't mind, I'm going to eat and then find my bed."

He left the room. His head hurt. He'd already talked more in the past hour than he had all week. People exhausted him. This one woman was worse than ten others.

THREE

"Don't mind him. He's been in a foul mood for years." Ariana watched Kat's brother—*Matt was his name, right?*—move around the corner and into the dining room. "I should apologize." She began untying her apron. "I was really out of line."

Kat stilled her hands.

"No. Let him get his dinner. Men are usually less grumpy after they eat. Let's clean up here and we can join him in a few minutes. Or, better yet, let's leave him alone, and we'll eat after he's finished."

Sighing, Ariana agreed. "All right." She re-tied her apron strings.

"So, where did you two meet?"

Blowing out a breath, Ariana faced Kat. "Earlier today. We had a brief encounter in the bakery."

"Leslie's?"

She nodded.

"Great scones." Kat placed a few sugar cookies in a box. "I'm assuming the meet did not go well."

"Let's just say it was...awkward."

"Hm."

"Uncle Matt hates Christmas." Aimee stood on a stool washing dishes at the sink. "I don't get it. He doesn't do presents, either."

"Aimee..." Kat gave her daughter a warning look.

"Well, he doesn't. He just sits in his house all alone on Christmas day and doesn't come eat with us, or anything."

The thought of anyone being alone on Christmas bothered Ariana. "Oh, Kat. That makes my heart hurt."

Sighing, Kat looked her way. "I know." Her voice lowered. "It's his own choice. He's a bit of a hermit. He works and goes home. Holidays, and especially Christmas, are not his best days."

Ariana glanced once more toward the dining room. "Well, I think that's awful. I just can't imagine...."

"There are reasons." Kat sidled around her and reached for a mixing bowl Aimee had placed in the dish drainer. She rubbed a dish towel over it.

"We don't talk about it," Aimee said.

"I can hear you," came a male voice from the dining room.

Ariana knew her eyebrows had probably shot up because she could feel the draw on her forehead from the inside. "I don't understand," she whispered, leaning toward Kat.

"Me either." Aimee shrugged.

Kat leaned closer, too. "It's not my story to tell. But I'll say this. It has to do with our parents and something that happened years ago."

"They died." Aimee whispered the words, then jumped down from the barstool, wiping her hands on a dish towel. "Done, Mom."

Kat bent to untie Aimee's apron strings. "Aimee...."

The little girl looked up at her mother with enormous eyes and whispered again. "Well, it's true."

"I'm so sorry to hear that." Ariana searched for some emotion on Kat's face, finding none.

Rising, Kat took a breath. "It was a long time ago." A tendril of hair slipped out of her barrette and she swiped it away from her face with her forearm. "But Ariana...?" She paused, searching her eyes, and then said softly, "He really is a good guy."

Reading more into the conversation from staring into Kat's eyes than by listening to her words, Ariana decided she would not press the matter any farther. "I'm sure he is, Kat," she whispered. "I just feel for him. And for you."

"All right. Enough." Matt shouted from the dining room. "I'm taking my dinner upstairs so you can talk about me without whispering."

Kat rolled her eyes. "Sleep well, Matt," she called out.

Ariana let out a breath—one she'd been holding forever, it felt like. "Well, that's that."

Kat agreed. "I think we're finished here." She took her own apron off and put her hand out for Ariana's. "Aimee, can you take these and put them in the laundry?"

"Yes, Mommy."

"Good. Let's get dinner."

It had been quite a while since her coffee and cookies earlier in the day. "Great. That beef and noodles dish has tickled my nose all afternoon."

But before they left the kitchen, Kat laid a hand on Ariana's forearm. "I know it's odd, and I'm saying more than I should, but Matt is the way he is because he's never been quite able to get over what happened. And this time of the year...well, it's just worse."

Studying Kat's face, Ariana saw the love and concern she

had for her brother. It was clear by her facial expression and the way she touched her just now. "I understand. I wish there were something I could do."

Kat shook her head. "Just be yourself, please? You are bright and cheerful and bubbly and so full life and the holiday spirit. We've needed a bit more Christmas spirit around here lately, and frankly, I think you may have been heaven sent to us this year."

Ariana stared, a little dumbfounded. "I can't imagine why, Kat. All I see around me is Christmas."

Exhaling long, Kat stepped closer. "Sometimes things aren't exactly as they seem, but we put up a good front."

Her words puzzled Ariana. "But—"

Suddenly, Aimee bounded back into the room. Kat rushed to her and pulled her daughter close. Smiling, she met Ariana's gaze again. "We are happy you are here. Come on. Let's eat."

Aimee looked up and grasped Ariana's hand. "I like you," she said.

Her heart swelled, and she felt so touched. "Oh, my. I like you too, sweet girl."

LATER, after dinner with Kat and Aimee, followed by cookies and cocoa by the fire in the living room, Ariana happily settled into her bedroom upstairs. She showered and slipped into her favorite flannel Christmas pajamas, pulled her laptop out of her bag, and tucked herself into her warm bed topped with a fluffy red and green quilted comforter. She smiled at the small Christmas tree in the corner of her bedroom. Its twinkling lights added a warm and festive ambiance to the room. It was the perfect atmosphere to jot down some highlights of her day, thinking about tomorrow's blog post.

She switched off the lamp beside her bed and worked only with the light from the laptop and the tree. The night before, she'd posted about her stay down the road. Her readers knew her destination was Dickens, and according to recent comments, they couldn't wait to learn more about the 'Official Christmas Village of New England,' as someone had once dubbed the town. Too tired to write the whole post now, she'd be ready by morning—if she had a few talking points to guide her.

Yawning, she typed a few notes about the town: the square and gazebo, the shops, Leslie's Bakes & More, the snow, and Holly Hill Inn. First impressions—maybe that's the focus of the piece. Her impressions of the town, the welcoming people like Kat and Aimee, and.... Her mind drifted and her eyes closed. When they did, behind her eyelids she saw the hardware store sitting undressed and plain among a town full of shiny balls and glittering tinsel—kind of like a wallflower sitting on a chair in the back of the dancehall, realizing she might never receive an invitation to dance.

And that reminded her of Matt. Her mind raced over all she'd learned about him today, their awkward conversations, and the not-so-positive interactions. Plus, Kat's words about him. *He really is a good guy.* All of it made her heart a little sad.

Kat was right. She shouldn't change who she was because of him. That would only depress her. She had to keep on doing her Christmas thing, as normal.

And Matt?

Well. Maybe she'd just have to ask him to dance.

Matt pushed back the curtains and peered out his bedroom window, watching the snow swirl around the security light pole below. It was early, but he was always up early, and old habits died hard. He rarely slept well when he was away from home but being back in his childhood bedroom had lulled him into a deep sleep.

He'd be ready for coffee soon, though.

Before leaving the store yesterday, he'd put a sign on the front door saying he was closed until after the first of the year. Probably shouldn't even have bothered with the looks of things outside. He doubted any of the shops would be open today—unless it would be the Old General Store and Post Office, both run by Hattie Howard, who had lived in the apartment above the store for the past forty years. She felt it her duty to be open every day—just in case someone needed something. Besides, neither snow nor sleet nor rain... Or whatever the saying was... The mail was always delivered.

Small town for sure, through and through.

Enough. Time for coffee.

The stairwell creaked as he descended. The Christmas tree was lit at the foot of the stairs, providing some light as he made his way down. He barely glanced at it as he passed. The only light in the kitchen came from a single under-the-cabinet fixture over the coffeemaker—a coffeemaker, which, to his delight, was on and brewing a fresh pot of coffee.

It didn't appear anyone else was up. Perhaps Kat prepared the coffee the night before and set the timer. Glancing at the clock on the stove, he realized it was barely six o'clock in the morning. His sister rarely slept in, but today, perhaps, she'd indulge herself.

The coffee finished, he reached for a cup, poured himself a mug, and leaned against the counter. One sip and his brain fog cleared.

It was unlike her not to be cooking breakfast, though—this was a bed-and-breakfast, after all—and she had a guest. But she knew what she was doing, and he would not wake her. This was her business. He didn't interfere.

The one guest.

He thought about the vivacious, Christmas-loving tourist he'd encountered yesterday. For some reason, she'd popped into his thoughts off and on since their first encounter. He couldn't imagine why. They obviously had nothing in common.

Hopefully, she would sleep late too. He wasn't up for merry, gleeful delight and unending Christmas cheer this morning.

He took his coffee and ambled toward the sunroom on the east side of the house. The morning sun—should it be able to penetrate the snow—would warm the room nicely on a day like this. He wandered through the family room and down the hall, then turned into the sunroom.

There was one low light on in the room, in the far corner next to the sofa. Someone else was up. The glow from a laptop screen lit up her face, and immediately he knew who was there. Ariana typed furiously, and obviously didn't realize he was there until he stepped inside and flicked on the overhead light. No way he was sitting in the near dark with her. That felt a little creepy and stalkerish—and the last thing he needed.

Her head jerked up, and a hand went to her chest. "Oh."

"Good morning." He took a sip of his coffee. "Sorry. I didn't mean to startle you. I didn't know anyone was in here." Something was different about her. Oh, yes. Glasses.

She bit her lip. "I was trying to be quiet."

"As a mouse, you were. I didn't mean to sneak up on you, either. Working?"

"Yes. Just finishing up, actually."

The conversation was a little stilted, but not necessarily unfriendly. Okay, he could do this. He headed toward an armchair. "Don't mind me. I'll just watch the snow and wait for the sun to come up." He sat and peered out the window, although there was not much to see, other than the blowing snow around the outside lights. Besides, it was still dark, and it appeared unlikely the sun would light or warm up the room today.

"Good luck," she said, maybe with a little sarcasm.

He chuckled a little inwardly. Pulling knitted throw from the back of the chair around his shoulders, he asked, "Are you chilly?"

She finished typing, then peeking over the laptop screen, pushed her glasses back up her nose and briefly met his gaze. "No. I'm fine. I have coffee to warm me up. Thanks." She gave him a half-smile.

"Hm." He noticed the mug of coffee on the side table to her right, and the small plate of cookies next to it.

Ariana went back to her work.

Closing his eyes, he listened to the gentle and rhythmic tap of her fingertips on the laptop keyboard. She'd feverishly type for a minute, then pause, then start in again. Something like that could lull a fellow back to sleep.

The clatter of her fingers stopped. A soft snap suggested she'd closed her laptop. Opening his eyes, he looked across the room.

She sat staring back, her coffee mug to her lips, and took a sip.

"Cookie?" She motioned to her plate. "I brought plenty."

His immediate reaction was to say no. Christmas cookie? No way. Then he looked at the pile of cookies on her plate and thought, *why not?*

"Sure." He got up and crossed the room. "What have you got there?"

"Pecan Meltaways, chocolate chip, and a fruitcake bar."

He took one of the powdered, sugar covered Meltaways. "I always loved these as a kid." He took a bite.

Ariana giggled.

"What?"

"Your shirt."

Looking down, he noticed the sugar dust on his chest. "Well, I look like a Christmas confection. Maybe you'll like me now." Immediately, he stepped back. Why those words came out of his mouth, he didn't know. Stupid. Glancing at Ariana, he caught her blank gaze, and then backed away. "I'll go back over here."

He did, and she scooted to the edge of the sofa.

"I don't *not* like you, Matt. I don't really know you."

Embarrassed, somewhat, he downplayed the situation. "I was joking, Ariana. See? I can have a funny, upbeat side of me too." *Badly played, but it was an attempt.*

"Sure. Hey. I should get back to my room." She began gathering her things. "I need to post this piece to my blog and do some other work stuff." She slipped her laptop into a bag at her feet, followed by a mouse and mouse pad. Then, pulling off her glasses, she snapped them inside a case and tossed them in the bag too. She rose and moved toward the door. "Enjoy your...um, sunrise?"

They both glanced out the window only to see blowing snow.

"Not happening." Matt stood. "I'm off to find Kat. She's usually up by now."

Ariana turned back at his words. "She's sleeping in this morning. I told her I didn't need breakfast. Hence, the cookies. She was exhausted last night."

Matt pondered that. Kat leave a guest to fend for herself? "That's unlike her."

"I insisted. Besides, it's Christmas Eve Eve. Everyone needs a down day occasionally. She's been going a mile-a-minute since I got here, and I have a feeling things will not let up for her until after the holiday."

"Yep. That's my sister." He thought for a second or two. "Christmas Eve Eve?"

"Yeah. It's a thing. In my world, anyway."

"Ah."

Ariana just stood and looked at him. After a moment, she faced him fully. "Matt, look. I want to apologize for yesterday. I think we started off on a bad note. I was, perhaps, a teeny bit rude, and...."

He stopped her by putting up a hand palm out. "No, I was the rude one. I was impatient standing in line yesterday and, in case you haven't noticed, I don't enjoy the holidays, so I was testy. Plus, I was hungry. So, it's all on me."

Still, she stared at him. "Not really. I appreciate it, but I goaded you a bit. Can we call a truce? Start over?"

Now it was his turn to stare. "I can do a truce. But that doesn't mean I still won't be grumpy."

Ariana laughed. "All right."

"But on one condition."

"Which is?"

"I want to like you, Ariana, so just don't push the Christmas stuff on me. Okay? That's going over the line."

Her eyes twinkled as she answered. "Oh, of course not, Matt. I wouldn't think of it."

FOUR

I *would just do it.*

Ariana smiled back at Matt. There would be no thinking, she was certain. If she pulled him kicking and screaming into Christmas, she would likely do it without rhyme or reason. She couldn't help it.

Christmas should be happy and spontaneous and giving. And like Kat said last night, she just had to be herself.

"There you two are. I wondered where you'd wandered off to."

Turning, Ariana saw Kat standing in the doorway. "I thought you were sleeping in?"

Kat looked at her watch. "Well, it's six-thirty in the morning and I'm usually up by five, so I say that's a rather good sleep-in. Are you two hungry?"

"I had cookies."

Kat looked at Matt's shirt. "Looks like you did, too."

"And coffee," he added.

"Well, that barely counts. Let's see what we can do. Besides, Aimee will be up soon, and she's cranky if she doesn't get a good breakfast. Plus, we have tons of things to do today—baking the gingerbread for the gingerbread house assembly tomorrow, prepping the cookie trays for tonight, and finish getting all the lights up in the house for the lighting—so let's get cracking."

Ariana watched Matt roll his eyes. "Tons of things to do that sound like Christmas—and we don't even know if anyone will be here for the lighting. As much as I would love to help with gingerbread and cookie arranging and the lights, I have some tasks I want to tend to, so...."

Kat stopped him with her glare. "Oh no. Not today, Mr. Pessimist. All the roads are closed, and the officials are telling everyone to stay in, so you're not going anywhere."

"My case in point."

Kat ignored him. "We are moving forward if there is a crowd, or not. It's—"

"Tradition. I know."

"And don't you think for one minute, Matt Matthews, that you are going to escape off to the attic or basement or barn to tinker, because today, in this house, it is all-hands-on-deck. Do you hear me?"

"Not sure what I can contribute, Kat."

"You're in charge of lighting."

"What? But you always take care of the lighting, and you are so particular."

"I'm going to be busy, Matt. Can you help, please?" She winked at Ariana.

Ariana truly had no clue what Kat was winking about, although she liked the way she handled her brother, and had rather enjoyed listening to their banter. She wondered if that was her usual modus operandi, or something new.

"I'm in," she said. "Just point me in the right direction. Matt? What do you say? We can do this. Right?"

"Is this a conspiracy?"

Kat shook her head. "No, this is family. Now, let's get breakfast and we can discuss."

Family?

Ariana warmed at the thought. Being part of a family like this would be wonderful. Not that her own family wasn't great —they were. And she loved her parents and sister more than anything. But this family—even with their quirks—just felt like....

Well, like her circle was complete.

How she could feel that way in such a short time—and with people she hadn't even known early yesterday—she didn't know.

About an hour later, Ariana peeked over Kat's shoulder at the list she was making while standing over the kitchen island. The three of them had breakfasted on sausage, eggs, and biscuits, and of course, more coffee. Aimee took sleeping in seriously and still wasn't up yet.

"So, this morning, Aimee and I will make the gingerbread dough and start baking the slabs so they will all be cool later today."

"Sounds good, Kat," Ariana said. "What can I do?" Then she glanced at Matt, who sat perched on a stool at the end of the kitchen island drinking coffee. "I mean, what can Matt and I do?"

He arched a brow.

Kat glanced sideways. "You two are going work on the window lights if you don't mind. I want something in every window."

Matt cleared his throat and glared at his sister. "Seriously? All the windows? Do you know how many that is?"

Pushing upright, she nodded. "Yes, I do. There are forty-two windows. I wash them every spring and fall. Since we can't do much outside other than what we have already done, let's focus on the house. I want a candle or maybe a wreath in every window. There are enough in the attic. Remember when Mom used to do that? Of course, I don't know if all the light bulbs still work so we will have to check them."

"Hm." Matt stared at the list.

"Okay?"

"Of course. What else?"

"I'm not sure," Kat said. "Do you two have any ideas?"

Ariana interrupted with a thought. "We have to be organized about this. I need to get a lay of the land and look at the windows. Where do you store your extra Christmas decorations, Kat?"

"Those are in the attic, too."

Ariana directed her attention to Matt. "Can we go look?"

Matt shoved off the island. "We have to go up there to get the candles, anyway."

"Great."

"What are you thinking, Ariana?"

Of course, she should tell Kat her idea. "Well, I'm just wondering if we can simulate a Christmas tree in some of the random windows, too. It would be more lights and maybe illuminate the house a bit more. But it should look balanced and not randomly chaotic." She watched Matt's face. He appeared to be thinking about that.

Matt crossed his arms. "Mom also used to put a small tree in some of the bedrooms."

"Like in my room! I love that," said Ariana.

"Yes." Kat grinned. "I love it, too. Can you two see what we have in the attic? I've not gone deep into the tree room in years."

The tree room? Ariana felt a little giddy. "Are you kidding?" She looked at Matt, stretching her eyes wider. "You have an honest-to-goodness Christmas tree room? Oh, point me in the right direction, please."

A hit of a smile crept across Matt's face. Ariana wondered if she amused him.

"This way," he said, turning away. Suddenly a crying Aimee appeared in the doorway, and he stopped short. "Aimee? What's wrong, sweetheart?"

She sailed past him and into her mother's arms. "Mommy!"

Her wail startled Ariana as she watched Kat scoop her up.

"Goodness, honey. What is the matter?" She held Aimee in her arms and sat her on the edge of the island. The little girl clung to her mother, her arms wrapped around her shoulders and her pajama-clad legs around Kat's waist.

"Dream," she finally said, hiccupping between words. "Bad. Daddy."

"Oh, honey..." Kat's eyes closed, and Ariana saw a tear escape a lower lid. At once, her heart went out to Aimee and her mom, and she wondered what in the world was going on.

Worried, she looked at Matt for some sort of answer. Instead, he crooked his finger for her to follow him, and then quickly and silently left the room.

She pursued him down the hallway and toward the entry, stopping at the base of the stairs.

"Matt?"

He put a finger to his lips. "Sh."

She nodded and whispered, "Okay."

Then he grabbed her hand and led her up the two flights of stairs to the attic.

Taking her hand had been bold of him—and to be honest, it was such an impulsive act that had he thought about it, he wouldn't have.

But he was glad he did.

It had been a long time since he'd held any woman's hand, and the feel of Ariana's small, soft palm in his was nice. Very nice. In fact, her fingers laced with his were pleasant enough that he slowed his steps as they approached the landing to the attic and was semi-reluctant to let go when they got there.

But just as quickly as he'd grabbed it, he released it.

The attic door creaked as he pushed it open. Moving past the threshold, he yanked an overhead pull string and light flooded the area. Before he could move farther inward, Ariana grasped his arm and stopped him.

"Matt?"

"Hm?"

"What was going on with Aimee? Seemed like more than a bad dream."

He perused Ariana's face. Her expression appeared full of concern and worry for his niece, and that touched his heart. Who was this woman who had suddenly burst into their lives? Someone who had him in the attic looking for Christmas decorations and felt genuine concern for his family?

"Yeah. Well, Dylan, Kat's husband, is deployed right now. He's on a mission and we don't know much. He's in the Navy, a SEAL. That, in and of itself, is stressful for Kat, as I'm sure you can understand. But right now, we're not sure where he is or when he's coming home. It's unlikely he will be here for Christmas."

"Oh, that's awful for a little girl."

"It's difficult for Kat, too. Although she understands Dylan's commitment. We're all proud of him. Aimee has been having a hard time because it's the first Christmas she won't see her daddy. And they've not been able to video call like they normally do."

"Poor baby."

"I know. I think Dylan being gone is one reason Kat keeps so busy. It keeps her mind off wondering where he is and if he's safe. It keeps Aimee's mind off it, too."

"Then we need to make sure this is the best Christmas ever, for Aimee and Kat." She stared at him, a dead serious look on her face.

Matt paused. "In case you haven't noticed, Christmas is not my forte."

"Really? Well then, it's a good thing it is mine."

He wanted to chuckle at her semi-amused expression, at the one cocked eyebrow and her slightly rounded lips. He couldn't help but grin at the twinkle in her big blue eyes. He had to admit she possessed an alluring charm that was sucking him right in. "All right. I'll make the effort. I can already see a plan forming in your head."

She laughed, but just as quickly, grew serious. Again, she touched his forearm. "No plan. Let's just make it a merry time. Matt, I came here because I wanted to write about the town of Dickens and experience a Dickens Christmas—but suddenly, I feel there is more here for me. I know this probably sounds odd, but I am drawn to your family and this place. And since I know my way around some Christmas decorations, I want to help make these next couple of days special. I need your help, though. Please? Let's do this for everyone. Even if it's just us here tonight."

He nodded. "Which is entirely likely."

Ariana blinked, looking up at him. "And that's really enough. Isn't it?"

He supposed it was. "All right. This way." He motioned and turned, still a bit in awe of Ariana. She'd fallen into their lives like a Christmas angel of hope and had suddenly changed the mood of this Christmas season—at least for him.

He led the way deeper into the attic. She followed, glancing about as they wove their way through boxes. "Wow. This *is* what you call a real attic."

Laughing, Matt headed to the right, where he knew the Christmas decorations were stored—or used to be anyway. "I suppose you don't have real attics in..." He stopped and turned. "Where are you from?"

"California."

For a moment, Matt studied her. "You drove all the way here from California?"

"Oh no." She began picking through a box of assorted Christmas paraphernalia. "I flew into Boston and rented a car. I've been in New England for a little over a week."

"And you're staying how long?"

She shrugged. "Through Christmas, at least. Longer, if the snow doesn't let up." She smiled warmly.

"But what about Christmas with your family back in California?"

"I'll miss it this year—and them—but I need to be here because this is where my writing brought me, and my writing pays the bills. My family understands my obsession with Christmas. Besides, there is no snow in So-Cal, and this year I want to be where the snow is."

"Well, you got that, for sure."

"I did."

"And you don't mind being stuck here for a few days longer than planned?"

"Mind? Oh, no. I'm ecstatic. I've never seen snow like this in my life."

She grinned wide and Matt smiled back.

There was something infectious about her enthusiasm. He

watched her turn back to the box and start poking through it. Matt realized he didn't mind watching her dig through the items. Their conversations were pleasant, too. Seemed they truly had called a truce.

"Oh, look at these..." Ariana peeled back an old quilt, covering the contents of a box, to reveal several wooden ornaments underneath. She picked up one and showed it to him. "These are gorgeous. Are they hand carved?"

Matt's gaze settled on the intricately carved snow scene on the wooden ball in Ariana's hands. His mind traveled back to a Christmas past, of the tree in the living room, tucked into the corner by the fireplace, and decorated with those old ornaments. When he and Kat were young, his parents, Ben and Jenny, didn't have a lot of money—most of what they made went back into the inn or the hardware—so they used what they had. These ornaments had been passed down from his dad's side of the family. He remembered how the lights on the tree would bounce off the wood and provide a warm glow in the room. It was a happier time.

"Yes. They are. My great-grandfather carved them, or so the story goes. I haven't seen these in years." He reached for the ornament and examined it, turning it over in his hands. "They still look good but could use a good polish. I can do that."

Ariana looked up, another ornament in her hand, and made eye contact. She appeared to be studying him now. "Are you okay, Matt?"

"Yes. Just memories." *Just a few ghosts of Christmas past.*

She held his gaze for another moment, then set the ornament back in place. "We could use these on the window trees if we can find them. Or perhaps the sunroom could use a tree. Over in the corner? What do you think?"

It was thoughtful of her to ask his opinion. "That would be

great. I've always liked these ornaments. It wouldn't hurt me to enjoy them again."

Ariana drew back, her eyes wide, and her mouth open. "You? Enjoy a Christmas something? My ears. What am I hearing?" Laughing, she softly punched his arm. "Just kidding, you know."

"Of course." And he didn't mind. Not really.

She spanned the attic then. "My goodness. Look at all the stuff in here." Turning, she eyed him again. "And no, I never lived in a house with an attic like this in California. We always lived in a ranch style home, which only had pull-down stairs in the ceiling that led to a place I never wanted to go. This..." She spun again, "is incredible."

"It's just a lot of old junk." Matt grinned.

"It's a lot of beautiful and interesting old junk. Oh look. I see lights over there."

Matt stood for a moment watching Ariana bounce from one thing to another. He had to smile at the joy she was getting from poking into all the assorted holiday trimmings. From boxes of greenery to a stash of red ribbons and bows to three more boxes of tree ornaments, and finally, to three plastic tubs full of electric candles and two spare boxes of light bulbs.

She was a refreshing beacon of light in his formerly dark and clouded world.

"Ariana? Thank you," he said aloud.

She looked up and caught his gaze. "For what?"

"For your efforts. Helping me see the joy of the season again."

Blinking, she held his gaze, and for once, it appeared she didn't know what to say. "Is it working?"

"Maybe a little. But Ariana, this is still difficult. I...."

She stood and approached him, touched his hand. "You don't have to explain, Matt. I don't want to push. You're welcome, of course, but if my obsessive enthusiasm about Christmas gets to be too much...."

"I will tell you."

"Good." She broke the connection between them and went back to rifling through a box of lights. "Now, if only those bulbs will work, *and* if we can find the little trees."

The serious mood broken, he stepped forward. "Over here." He knew exactly where those were. Leading her to the side of the attic, he opened another door and ducked to step inside. "Watch your head."

Ariana followed. "Wow."

"You keep saying that."

"Because... Wow. Is this the tree room?"

He swept an arm toward the center. "Yes. You asked for Christmas trees, madam? Here you go."

"And all shapes and sizes." She whipped back, her wide-eyed gaze landing on him. "We have our work cut out for us. How many windows again?"

Matt laughed out loud. Watching her was like watching a kid in a penny candy shop—and for some reason, that gave him a bit of joy. "Forty-two. And yes. That, we do. I'm at your command."

She sailed off to inspect the trees. Whether or not he wanted to admit it, he was enjoying this day, and being with Ariana.

ARIANA FELT both overwhelmed and excited. "So, we really get to decorate with all of this stuff?"

"Any and all of it. Whatever you want to use," Matt told her.

"I'm hoping I don't bite off more than we can chew... But Matt, I want to use it all."

"All of it?"

"I have ideas running through my head. Brilliantly, beautiful Christmas ideas."

"Oh, boy."

She twisted back. "I thought you were going to say *Bah, Humbug*, and I was about to chuck this ball of tinsel at you."

"Naw. I think my inner Scrooge is still sleeping in today, for some odd reason."

"Good. Keep him there."

"I'll try."

Ariana caught his eye. There he was again, just looking at her like she was this odd character or something. "So, okay, I know I'm weird about Christmas."

He shook his head. "No. You are incredibly bubbly and energetic about Christmas. Nothing weird about it at all. I think I'm the weird one."

"I think you're softening."

"I think you may have something to do with that."

Her heart kicked up a beat and that startled her a little. She turned away, ignoring the heart-thumping thing. "Then my job here is done." *Or maybe just beginning.* Ariana hesitated and looked at him again.

His gaze skittered over her face.

A switch had flipped a minute ago. Why was her heart fluttering wildly in her chest just now? *Not thinking about that.*

"I'd say we're off to a good start."

She nodded and dismissed her wayward thoughts.

"Agreed. Before we drag stuff downstairs, I want to get a look at all forty-two of those windows. Maybe make some sketches and a plan."

"Sounds good." Matt reached for the two boxes of light

bulbs and a box of candles. "I'm going to take these with us so I can test out these bulbs."

"Great idea. Let's get started."

He led the way out of the attic. Ariana followed, watching Matt carry the boxes down the stairs, wondering why all at once she felt a little different toward him. Somehow, in such a short time, her feelings for him had done an about face, swinging from empathy to... To something different.

FIVE

Ariana stepped back and perused the arrangement. It was the last one she'd pulled together, and this one was simple—a single candle, some holly, and a red bow. The window was situated in a short hall off the entry, leading into the dining room. With all the decorations in the rooms on either side, she didn't feel they needed to go overboard in this spot.

The aroma of gingerbread wafting down the hallway tickled her nose and teased her appetite, leaving her with a warm, cozy, Christmassy feeling. Hours had passed since breakfast and her tummy was growling, so she hoped to grab something to eat soon. Plus, the scents of cinnamon, nutmeg, and ginger weren't helping matters any. She tilted her head to one side, satisfied the uncomplicated approach there was perfect, and nothing else needed to be added.

Matt stepped up beside her. "That looks nice."

"I think so, too."

"I secured all the candles in the sunroom windows," he

added. "Thanks for getting the greenery ready there. The sunroom is going to look awesome tonight."

She glanced his way. "I love the addition of the tree in the corner. The colors will pop through the windows. Plus, those wooden ornaments look even more awesome since you polished them. They really seem to glow. I can't wait to get pictures of everything."

He moved closer. "You've done a great job in the sunroom, Ariana. Aimee and Kat are going to love it."

That was certainly her intent. "It was fun. If it's the one place we can keep Aimee out of until tonight, that would be great."

"I was just in the kitchen. I think they will be busy for a while longer."

"Good." She stared at the window for another few seconds, cocking her head to the side, and studying it from all angles. "If I can get a good picture of this, it will be great for my blog post tomorrow."

Matt stood silent beside her.

After a moment, the stillness between them felt awkward. The atmosphere crackled between them a little. She peeked his way. The smile he wore earlier had dissipated. "Matt?"

"Hm?"

"Everything okay? You have a look."

He shook himself and stepped forward to fiddle with the candle. "I'm fine. Glad those bulbs worked."

Ariana wasn't so sure, but she would not push it. "Me too. I can't believe you had all those extras in your truck. I mean, who would have thought?"

He chuckled. "I know my sister. I grabbed those before I left the store, just in case."

Glad to see him smile again, she faced him, crossing her

arms over her chest. "So. You actually have some Christmas decorations in that store of yours."

"They were tucked in the back room, left over from when Dad managed the store and Mom had her art studio there. She would create all sorts of Christmas scenes for the inn, the hardware store, and the town. She'd paint the characters and use the lights to illuminate." He stared out the window for a moment, thinking back, perhaps. "The lights were old, that's why I wanted to test them first."

"I see. Makes sense."

He stood for a moment, looking past Ariana. "They've been gone a while, my parents, but both of them have been on my mind a lot today."

Maybe that's why his attention keeps drifting. "That's understandable, Matt. I'm sorry. Kat mentioned yesterday they were no longer living."

He said nothing for a minute. "You know, for a long time I avoided Christmas because it dredged up too many memories, too much emotion. Sometimes, I just couldn't handle all the feelings. You'd think at my age, and after all this time, I'd have dealt with it—but I haven't. Not really. Yet today, I welcomed the memories."

Ariana moved closer and touched his forearm. "That sounds encouraging, Matt."

He made eye contact and Ariana's heart warmed at the connection. "I hope so."

She held his stare a little longer. "How long have they been gone, Matt?" The instant she said the words, she wondered if her question was out of line. A sliver of panic raced over her abdomen. "I'm sorry. I shouldn't have...."

His gaze moved from hers, now transfixed on the candle. Matt seemed far away again. Ariana waited while he gathered his thoughts—and maybe his emotions—then briefly made eye contact and turned toward the entryway.

"A long time." He took a couple of steps and paused, as if contemplating whether he wanted to continue that line of conversation. He faced Ariana. "I've never seen two people enjoy each other so much—practically inseparable and so much in love. They shared an incredibly strong bond. And they loved Christmas." He smiled then, for a moment, his gaze back in sync with Ariana's. "They got married on Christmas day."

Ariana smiled. "I can't think of a more beautiful day to get married."

Their gazes danced then. "Maybe someday I'll tell you their story."

"I would like that."

He heaved a sigh and tossed another glance toward the entryway. "How about we check on the gingerbread girls?"

"Sure."

Ariana watched him move away. His off-and-on somber mood tugged at her heart. She wished she'd not asked that question but at least Matt had shared something personal. That was positive, she hoped.

Her thoughts wandered back to what Kat said the night before. *It's not my story to tell.* So, if Matt wanted her to know more, he'd tell her. She just had to be patient.

He turned. "You coming? I'm starved." He reached for her hand.

Instinctively, she stepped forward and met his grasp, and their fingers mingled for a few seconds. "Yes. But I want to run up to my room and get my camera first. I'll just be a few seconds."

She dropped his hand and tore her gaze away as she started for the stairs. A cool draft of air swept down the staircase as she ascended, causing her to shiver. Yet, his touch still lingered warm and inviting on her fingertips.

THE SMELL of baking gingerbread was even more overpowering in the kitchen than throughout the rest of the house. Ariana immediately began snapping pictures of Kat and Aimee as they baked. Aimee kneeled on a stool at the kitchen island—a pillow under her knees—rolling out gingerbread dough. She wore a too-big apron wrapped around her waist and tied in the front. She wore flour smudges on her cheeks, dough on her fingers, and a smile on her face. Glancing up as Ariana aimed the camera her way, she smiled a big, toothless grin. Ariana snapped the picture.

"That one is awesome."

Aimee grinned wider. "We've been baking all day."

"I know. I could smell the ginger all over the house." Ariana stepped closer to the island. "Are you tired?"

"A little. Mostly, it's fun."

"She was a big help today," Kat called out from across the room. She peeked into the oven. "Just a couple more minutes on this one. We'll finish soon."

Ariana snapped another picture of Kat. Then, looking about, she noticed all the gingerbread layers cooling on racks. "Goodness. When did you say the gingerbread house assembly happens?"

"Tomorrow," said Aimee. "We always do it on Christmas Eve. It's—"

"Tradition." All voices in the room chimed in at once. Including the male voice coming from the breakfast nook, which was decidedly the loudest.

Aimee giggled. "Uncle Matt. You're funny."

He rose from the table, a sandwich plate in hand, and reached over to pinch Aimee's nose. "And don't you forget it, elf."

"I'm not an elf." Aimee giggled some more and batted at his hands.

Ariana snapped a quick picture of the interaction between the two.

Matt turned to Ariana. "Sandwich fixings are on the table." He dusted the crumbs off his plate into the garbage and stashed the plate in the dishwasher. "Still hungry?"

"Famished. Thanks."

"No problem." Brushing his hands together, he added, "I've got some things to take care of outside—looks like the snow has stopped for a while—I'll be in the barn if either of you need me."

Kat turned. "In the barn? Are the lights finished?"

Matt approached his sister and gave her a peck on the cheek. "Relax. All done, sis. And you can thank Ariana for the expertise. It's going to look great tonight and I can't wait for you to see it. However, we're requesting no peeking until later. Okay? That includes both you and the elf." He ticked his head toward Aimee.

"I'm not an elf, Uncle Matt!"

"What?" He turned and swept Aimee off the chair and swung her around. "I'm sure your ears are pointed. Let me see." Sitting her back down on the stool, he went about inspecting her ears. "Hm..." he said softly. "I thought I saw points there last year. Maybe they don't come out until Christmas Eve."

Aimee giggled again. "I don't have points, Uncle Matt."

He shrugged. "Well, let's wait and see tomorrow. I do think I see little ear buds starting to grow, though. You better go look in a mirror."

"What?" A wide-eyed Aimee hopped off the bar stool and ran out of the room.

Kat wiped her hands on a dish towel, tossed a quick glance at Ariana, and then gave Matt a long, hard look. "Excuse me. Who are you and what have you done with my brother?"

Matt feigned innocence. "What?"

Smiling, Ariana shrugged. "This guy sort of appeared this afternoon."

Kat faced Matt and gave him a bear hug. "Well, I like him."

Rolling his eyes at Ariana, he hugged his sister back, then settled his hands on her shoulders and gently pushed away. "Let's forgo the mushy stuff."

Kat grinned ear to ear.

Matt's phone binged. He fished it out of his pocket, glanced at the face, and then turned away from the women. "Gotta take this. Later."

"Dinner is at six." Kat called out. "And then the lighting."

Waving with one hand, he headed down the hall, his phone to his ear.

"Well, that's that," Ariana said. She watched him disappear down the hallway. Her heart felt light and happy for Matt. And, for herself. She liked him, despite his quirks, and wanted him to be happy.

"And he's been like this all afternoon?"

"Off and on." She swiveled to look at Kat. "He's had a few nostalgic moments mixed in, I guess you would call them, but he was okay. It surprised me he didn't balk at anything. We worked very well together."

"Great!"

Ariana picked up a peppermint disc. "These look so festive."

"Thanks. I love doing them."

"Matt told me a little about your parents a few minutes ago."

Kat swiveled to look at her, putting down her spatula. "Did he say much?"

"Only that he's having pleasant memories today. Oh, and he talked a little about them, about how much in love they were."

Kat's eyes misted over. "They were incredible." Moving closer, she added, "I told you he was a good guy."

"I know. He is." Ariana gave her a quick hug, then glanced down the hallway where Matt had gone. "I like him."

Returning to her gingerbread, Kat smiled. "I think the feeling is mutual."

Ariana's attention shifted. "What? I certainly didn't mean, well, you know, romantically."

The smile on Kat's face widened. "Why not? Romance has to start somewhere."

"I didn't come here for romance, Kat. I came to work. And while I'm sure that Matt is a great guy, and he is personable, and I did enjoy spending time with him, I don't feel...." Her words tapered off. How did she feel?

"Well, I think there is something between you two. I can see it."

"Really?"

"He likes you, Ariana. And you said you like him. So, what does it hurt to explore a relationship? Besides, you are good for him."

"He's fine figuring things out on his own, Kat."

Shrugging, Kat faced her. "Maybe. His track record isn't so great. I think it's you. I've tried to pull him into Christmas without success. You pop in here for a day or two and suddenly he's digging into the tree room and hanging garland."

"Oh no. It's not me. I think he's just ready to leave whatever it is behind."

"Maybe." Kat grasped Ariana's hand. "But I still think it's you." Kat squeezed her hand, then headed to the oven. "So, what is this about not looking at the lights in the sunroom?"

"Well, do you mind keeping Aimee out of the sunroom until the lighting? You, too. Okay?"

Kat gave her the side-eye and crossed her arms. "But I need to set up the cookie trays. We always have cookies and cocoa in there after the lighting."

"I'll get everything set up for you."

Kat paused. "Actually, with finishing up here and trying to get dinner on, that would be awesome. Are you sure you don't mind?"

"Are you kidding me? I live for this stuff."

"Oh, that's right. Silly me." Amused, she added, "You know where the cookies are. The fancy trays are in the built-in cupboard in the dining room." She checked the oven. "Oh, and check the bottom section of the hutch in the sunroom. I have a few decorations stashed there that I've used in the past. Help yourself. Whatever you need."

"Great. I'm on it. Right after a sandwich."

"Mom! Ariana!" Aimee burst back into the room. "Uncle Matt lied! I don't have ear bugs! Look!"

Kat and Ariana burst out laughing.

Aimee parked her hands on her hips. "Stop laughing at me!"

Kat's lips clamped up tight, and Ariana had to swallow a giggle. The little girl was so darned serious that it made Ariana's stomach hurt from holding in her laughter. Finally, she gained control and crouched to meet Aimee's gaze. "I think Uncle Matt was teasing you, sweetheart."

Aimee rolled her eyes and shrugged. "I dunno what's up with him!"

"Aimee Hall? I can use your help over here," Kat called out.

"Coming..."

Ariana watched Kat bustle about. "Matt told me about your husband being deployed. I'm sorry to hear that."

Kat's hands stilled, her eyes closed, and she exhaled. "I'm trying not to think about it."

Ariana stepped closer. "And I just made you think about it. I'm sorry about that too. But Kat, you need to slow down. You can't fill every minute of the day with activity just so you don't think about it."

Kat looked ahead for a few seconds, then dropped her gaze to her daughter sitting at the island, busying herself sorting candies. "I know. But it's better than drinking. Right?" She faked laughter.

Ariana touched Kat's hand.

Kat eyes grew misty. "I don't want to upset Aimee," she whispered.

Ariana nodded. "I understand."

THE SUNROOM WAS LIT up and glowing. The lights from the candles and the Christmas tree bounced off the floor-to-ceiling windows on three walls, only adding to the magical effect. From the inside looking out, the reflections amplified the amount of light in the room. Ariana perused every nook and cranny—she wasn't sure she could get more Christmas in the room if she tried.

Trays of cookies sat on end tables and the coffee table, as well as on the buffet top of a built-in hutch to her left. Also there, sat two thermoses of hot cocoa, a pitcher, and assorted candy additions for the hot chocolate, such as marshmallows, red hot candies, candy canes, and other chocolate meltables. She'd pulled fancy dessert plates and cups from the cupboard in the dining room, along with some candlestick holders and candles. She had forks and spoons and stirrers and napkins, too. All she needed to do later was to light the candles.

Except. No. Not quite finished yet.

Ariana glanced about one last time.

If she had some glass ornaments, they would go perfectly in the wooden bowl over on that side table. And if she could find some tinsel, she could tie it around the candlesticks. And....

Oh. She snapped her fingers. Kat said there were decorations. Ariana's gaze swept to the bottom of the hutch.

Crouching there, she opened the doors and pulled out a few boxes.

There. Some tinsel.

Oh, this holly will work great.

And some glass balls. Perfect.

Taking what she needed and setting them aside, Ariana set the boxes back on the shelf. When she did, a framed photograph dislodged and fell out. She caught it before it hit the floor.

Turning the frame over, she ran a finger over the dusty glass. The image was several years old, to be sure. The photograph was of a family standing in front of the inn. There was snow on the ground and the house was lit up behind them, as was the picket fence and arch.

There were four people. Two adults, two children. A boy and a girl.

"Kat and Matt?"

She thumbed over them, wiping away more dust. "Yes." And their parents, she guessed.

Kat looked to be in her young teens, Matt a couple of years younger. Everyone was smiling. Happy.

Turning the frame over, she read the words scrawled on the backing. *The Holly Hill Inn Christmas Lighting, 2005. Ben, Jenny, Kat, and Matt Matthews.*

Ariana took a deep breath. Glancing into the cabinet, she located a dust cloth and cleaner. Quickly, she swiped the frame and picture, and set it atop the buffet. Then, she went about placing the final touches around the room—some holly on the hutch, tinsel on the candlesticks, ornaments in the bowl.

With one last glance about the room, she made a quick decision to place the picture on the hutch—front and center and eye level—where it would surely be noticed when people got their hot cocoa.

Stepping back, she smiled. What a lovely tribute to this family and the inn.

Her heart felt full, and she was excited for the evening to come. With a lingering over-her-shoulder perusal, she left the room to change for dinner.

SIX

"Why can't we go out on the porch?" Aimee looked up at her mom. "Why can't I go in the sunroom? And why are all the lights turned off inside?"

"Because Uncle Matt said so, and he told us to stay here in the entryway and wait for him. Patience, little one."

Ariana smiled at the anxious child. "The surprise will be so much better if you wait," she told Aimee.

The girl rolled her eyes and did a little jiggly dance. "But I am patient...."

"*Im*patient." Kat looked down at her daughter.

"Oh look. I see lights." Aimee jumped and pointed out the door window. "Is that Uncle Matt?"

Ariana watched as a vehicle drove up from barn area, circled the drive, and parked in front of newly shoveled sidewalk. The snow had stopped earlier in the afternoon—which was a godsend—and Matt had shoveled the drive and walks, and then worked in the barn throughout the afternoon. In fact, he didn't even come in for dinner.

"I can't believe it." A wide-eyed Kat glanced at Ariana. "Do you know anything about this?"

"No. I'm as clueless as you."

"I think I'm witnessing a miracle," Kat added.

Ariana noticed tears in Kat's eyes. "Hey, are you okay?"

In the next motion, Kat embraced Ariana and held her tight. "Thank you," she said. "Thank you."

"But I did nothing." Ariana pulled back and looked into Kat's eyes.

"You've done more than you know."

The door swung open. Matt stood framed in the doorway, then glanced to his right, tapped something on the wall outside the door, and stepped inside.

"Uncle Matt!" Aimee excitedly flew forward. "Are we ready now?"

He swept her up into his arms. "We are, elf. Let's go."

Ariana watched as he paused briefly, held Kat's tearing gaze for a moment, and reached out to touch her shoulder. Then, just as quickly, he stepped away.

"This way, folks. Follow me. Watch for icy snow on the bricks."

He carried Aimee and walked ahead. Kat locked arms with Ariana and they made their way down the porch steps and along the brick walk to where Matt had parked. It was dark, the sun had set about thirty minutes earlier, but the porch light and an outside lantern lit their way—plus the outside security lights away from the house. When they were all there, Matt lowered Aimee to the ground and turned to the pair.

Kat stepped forward. "Matt. How did you get this old thing running again?"

He shrugged. "Luckily, with a little tinkering and some good gas, she started right up." He glanced at the truck. "But I didn't want to risk turning her off again, so that's why I left her idling."

Ariana looked at the old pickup truck. She knew nothing about trucks, but as far as this one went, it was charming, to be sure. Red with white wooden side-rails, with the words Holly Hill Inn painted on the passenger side door. "What a cute truck."

"It's a 1956 Ford F100. A classic. I'm just glad she started."

Ariana laughed. "All of those words and numbers mean nothing to me, but I still think she is adorable."

"This was our father's truck," Kat said. "At least the one he bought to showcase the inn. Every truck he ever owned was red. He bought this one in the 90s, restored it himself, then drove it every day until... Well, until he didn't. But on the evening of the lighting, we had a tradition."

Matt nodded, glancing to his watch. "Yes, and we need to quit standing out here in the cold and get to that tradition." He reached for Ariana's hand. "Do you mind sitting in the middle, Ariana? Kat, sit by the door with Aimee on your lap."

They all scrambled into the truck cab. Matt rounded the front and got in beside Ariana. When he did, they made eye contact for a moment. "You're full of surprises," she told him.

He patted her knee, leaned closer, and whispered, "Just wait."

Ariana's heart fluttered at his closeness. "So, about this tradition?" She directed that to Kat.

Matt put the truck into drive.

"Well, before the guests would come for the lighting, Dad would pile all of us in the truck, just like now, and we would drive around the property looking at the house from all angles." She stopped talking and leaned forward to look out the windshield. "Matt, did you snowplow this path today?" She glanced sideways at him.

"I did."

"Just like dad."

Ariana looked back and forth between them.

"Yep. I guess so."

Kat's eyes welled up again. Ariana reached out and clasped her hand. Kat squeezed it tight.

Matt drove toward the back of the inn, circled around, and parked the truck so they could get the full and unobstructed view of the back of the house and the side garden.

"Wait for it." He pushed his coat sleeve back to look at his watch.

"What?" Kat glanced his way.

"Now."

At once, the entire house lit up like a burst of fireworks. Lights twinkled on the trees and holly bushes outside the inn, skittered along the picket fence, and raced up and over the arch. To Ariana, the most beautiful part was the candles dancing in all the windows, like little punctuation marks of prettiness. The sunroom was especially magnificent.

She gasped. "That is splendidly beautiful."

Matt exhaled, and Ariana looked his way. He stared straight ahead, and she noticed that his eyes, too, had grown misty. He turned her way.

"Dad was all about the dramatic," he said. "The flare. He was ahead of his time with electronics and he loved to tinker. Running the hardware store was perfect because he had access to all kinds of gadgets and tools and devices. When there was downtime, he was fiddling with something. One year, he rigged up the lighting system in the entire house—inside and out—to come on and off with a series of timers. I had no clue if it would still work, but by Christmas, it did."

Ariana sighed and looked again at the inn. "By Christmas, you are right."

"Well, it's beautiful," Kat said. "And that sunroom literally pops."

Aimee bounced on her mother's lap. "I see a tree in there." Her eyes grew wide.

"Yes, we added a few trees here and there," Ariana told her. "It's lovely."

"It's magic." Ariana whispered the words and stared ahead. She, too, felt a little like crying. "Thank you both for letting me be a part of this day." Suddenly, she knew she had found the perfect Christmas, and it wasn't in Dickens—it was here at Holly Hill Inn. Christmas wasn't only about tinsel and snow globes and mistletoe—it was about family and relationships.

While she knew that, being with Kat and Aimee and Matt, and being privy to their family struggles, made her not only appreciate the holiday and her own family but differently.

Matt fumbled for her hand and clasped it tight. He'd taken off his glove, and Ariana welcomed the warmth of his fingers wrapped around hers, not to mention his affection. That warmth and affection traveled from her hand right up to her heart. Slowly turning, she met his searching gaze.

"Thank you," he whispered back.

The moment was suspended for a heartbeat or two.

"Is that a light coming up the road?"

Matt quickly released Ariana's hand and pulled the truck out of park and into reverse, again glancing at his watch. "Crap. Yes, it is."

"We have guests?"

Ariana was confused. "I thought the roads were still closed."

Matt drove slowly to the front of the property. "They were earlier, but there are ways to get through. If there is a will..." As they grew closer, everyone in the truck's cab grew silent.

"There is a way. Dylan always says that. Oh my God. Matt? What have you done?"

Ariana watched him shrug, then catch his sister's questioning gaze. "I just helped Santa a bit."

"It's not a car. It's a sleigh. Is it Santa?"

Ariana followed Aimee's gaze and immediately felt her bouncing excitement. As they pulled up closer to the front of the inn, she noticed a driver—who happened to look a lot like Santa—help a man get his gear out of the sleigh and onto the ground.

A man who was wearing a military uniform.

Aimee screamed, "It's my daddy!"

"Oh my God." Kat burst into tears.

Matt parked the truck. Kat's door flew open. Aimee jumped out and ran. Kat let go a sob, looked again at Matt, and then followed behind her daughter at a slower pace.

Ariana sat in the truck with Matt, tears in her eyes, and watched the reunion scene unfold before her. Dylan Hall hugged and kissed his wife, pulling her close with one arm, while holding his daughter with the other. After a moment, Ariana turned to Matt...who was looking back at her.

"You did this?"

He shook his head. "No. Dylan did this. I just helped him set the scene, a little."

"You have a good heart, Matt Matthews," she said. "You are a good man."

Matt's gaze traveled over her face and landed on her lips. One hand cupped her cheek as he leaned in, searched her eyes momentarily, and then placed a soft, sweet, kiss on her mouth.

Their lips danced for a few seconds. His lingered over hers with featherlike touches. Then he gently pulled back.

Ariana sighed and closed her eyes at this release of lips.

Matt's arms went around her and tugged her closer.

Wrapped up in his embrace, her head against his chest, his heart beating wildly against her cheek, Ariana had never been more content in her life.

Walking slowly into the inn, holding hands with Ariana, Matt felt on top of the world. He paused for a moment at the entrance, tapped the Holly Hill Inn sign next to the door, and glanced to Ariana.

"I noticed Kat do that the other day. And you, earlier. Why?"

He ran his hand over the old sign. The wood was weathered, and the painted lettering had faded, but both he and Kat had hesitated to have it repainted. "Mom and Dad put this sign here the year they opened the inn," he told Ariana. "Since they've been gone, tapping the sign is something we both do, sort of like saying hello to our parents."

Ariana squeezed his hand and stepped closer. "That's lovely." She trailed a finger over the letters and read the words below the name of the inn. "In loving memory of Elaine and Harold Peterson." She looked at Matt. "Who are they?"

"They owned the farm before my parents. Elaine willed the farm to them when she died in 1990. There is a whole story about how my parents and the Peterson's are connected that I'll tell you one of these days." He looked down at her and grinned. "It's a story about love and commitment, about holding on and letting go."

Ariana's head bobbed up and down. "Oh. Tell me later?"

He leaned closer and kissed the tip of her nose. "I would love to."

They slowly moved inside, following a chatty Aimee into the large entryway. The animated girl engaged her dad in

66

excited conversation, while a quiet Kat clung to Dylan's arm listening to every word her husband and daughter said.

The trio hurried down the hallway and turned right.

"They are so happy." Ariana slipped out of her coat and boots and looked up at him. "I need to run upstairs and get my camera."

"Can't it wait?" His hands lingered at her waist. Her full lips looked like they needed kissing again.

She shook her head. "Oh no. I want to capture their expressions from the beginning when they step into the room." She broke away.

Matt stopped her with a hand to her cheek. "Wait."

Her eyes grew round. "Oh?"

"Your mouth needs nibbling," he said.

"It does?"

Pulling her into his embrace once more, he brushed his lips over hers and then deepened the kiss. His heart sang as her arms went around his neck and she solidly kissed him back.

Pulling away slowly, she peered into Matt's eyes. "More of those later?"

He grinned. "Oh, yes."

"Good. Because right now we need to get in that sunroom."

He dropped his arms. "All right."

"And I need my camera."

Matt frowned a little and watched her fly up the stairs. He wasn't sure he understood this blogging business and the need for pictures, but it seemed important to her. Her feet padded quickly along the carpeted hallway overhead, entered her bedroom, and then reversed. She came flying back down the stairs as quick as she'd left.

"Hurry," she said. "I want to see their faces when they see the lights."

"Yes. Of course."

They hustled down the hall and burst into the sunroom. Aimee twirled, eyes wide, her gaze shooting about, looking at everything. Matt watched Ariana aim her camera and snap picture after picture as an excited Aimee delightfully chattered with her parents as she took in all the Christmas cheer.

Matt had to admit the room looked awesome—lights twinkling and reflecting, the cookies, the decorations. Ariana had evidently added a few more touches after he'd finished with the candles.

Dylan and Kat settled onto the sofa. Aimee plopped down with them looking at the cookies. "I want one of those, and one of these, and oh, one of those too."

"Slow down there, little one. There will be plenty. You don't have to eat them all tonight."

"I know." She turned toward her dad. "We have to save some for Santa tomorrow."

"Absolutely.

Dylan winked at Kat.

Aimee reached for a cookie. "Can I have some cocoa too?"

"Of course, you may," Kat told her.

"I'll get it, elf." Matt turned toward the buffet. "I'm closer."

"Thanks, Matt."

"I'll help," Ariana said.

Matt glanced her way, tossing her a covert grin as she joined him. He liked that they shared this little kissing secret between them, and he wasn't ready to share it with anyone else yet. It was nice that it was just the two of them.

But when he reached the buffet, he halted, their stolen kisses forgotten. His gaze focused on a picture on the hutch—one he knew wasn't there earlier—one he hadn't seen in an awfully long time. "What is this?" He flipped around, looking at Kat. "Why is this here?"

"What do you mean?"

"You know what." He pointed. "This picture."

ARIANA WATCHED the unfolding scene as if it were happening in slow motion.

Kat headed toward the hutch—her gaze connected with Matt's. Her expression puzzled. "I don't know. What picture is it?"

Then she stopped up short, too. "Oh."

Ariana froze. From the looks on their two faces, she knew she'd made a mistake. "It was me. It's a lovely picture, and I thought it would be nice to display, but I'm sensing I was wrong. I'm so sorry."

They turned and stared.

Ariana took a step forward. "I found it in the lower buffet cabinet. The note on the back said—"

"We know what the note says." Matt snatched the picture off the shelf and shoved it back into the cabinet. Rising, he looked Ariana square in the eyes. "You have no right to butt into our family business."

"Matt!" Kat grasped his arm.

Dylan rose and headed toward the door with Aimee in his arms. "We are going to take an exit," he said. "To see if there are more cookies and cocoa in the kitchen."

"Good idea." Matt stared at Ariana. "Aimee doesn't need to hear what I am about to say."

Ariana was floored. "Matt, please. I thought it was a beautiful family picture and—"

"And it was not up to you to decide to put it there."

"I thought you'd like your parents to be... Earlier today, you mentioned them and I thought you would be open to having them be a part of tonight's lighting, kind of like with the truck and the lights and..." She stepped talking, searching his face. "I was wrong. Matt, I'm sorry."

His expression was stern, emotionless, unmoving. "That's enough. You've come in here with your glitter and sparkle and upbeat attitude and you think you can make everything all right with a few baubles and some candy canes. You can't. Nothing can change the past, Ariana. Not even an old picture that should never see the light of day again."

"But Matt. It's your family."

"Was my family."

"They are still your family."

He stepped closer. "All you care about is getting your Christmas pictures for your blog or article or whatever. You want to portray the perfect Christmas, the perfect town, the perfect inn, the perfect family. Well, that's not us, so put your camera away. Besides, I hate all this commercial Christmas crap anyway."

She looked at Kat. "No. It's not like that. It was never like that."

Matt pushed past her. "Oh, I'm sure it is."

"I'm so sorry. I don't know what I've done wrong."

Kat touched her shoulder.

He headed for the door. "I'm going to the farm."

Rushing after him, Kat called out. "Matt, the roads."

"I'll be fine."

Ariana moved past Kat and followed Matt down the hall and into the entryway. "Matt, please. Can we talk about this? I don't know what I did wrong, but I want to understand and apologize and make it right."

He looked up as he grabbed one of his boots and shoved a foot into it. "I've been a fool. Just got caught up in the magic of it all. Magic isn't real. Christmas isn't real. *You and I are not real*, no matter how much I—" He cut his words short and glanced off. "Nothing can bring them back. Not a picture. Not a memory. They are gone and you can't fix that."

She halted, stunned by his words. *They* weren't real? "I didn't want fix anything, Matt. I can't. But I believe that you can keep their memories alive in your heart. You just have to believe that, too. Heck, you do that every time to you tap the sign at the door."

He glared. "You don't get to talk about that." He shoved his other foot in his boot now and grabbed his coat. "I don't believe in any of this. I told you that from the beginning."

"And I don't believe *that* for a minute." She lifted her chin in defiance.

"Well, you don't have to." He quickly zipped his coat. "Be careful traveling home, Ariana. I hope you got what you came for."

He left, slamming the door a little too hard behind him. She jumped. Tears filled her eyes as she watched his shadow stalk down the brick walk and across the parking area to his truck.

"I didn't know..." she whispered. "I'm so sorry."

Turning, she noticed Kat standing beside her. "You did nothing wrong."

"I need to go after him." She bolted forward.

Kat grasped her arm. "No. Let him go."

Whirling back, she looked Kat square in the eyes. "I need to explain. We can't let him just go off like this. Things just feel...undone."

Kat held Ariana by both shoulders and gave her a little shake. "Ariana, this is Matt's problem to work out. Not yours. And not mine either. You and I have both done all we can. He's the one who has to work through these issues."

"And what issue are those, Kat?"

She glanced off and exhaled. "The picture triggered a terrible memory."

"How was I to know?"

"You couldn't. But it *was* in the cabinet for a reason. I put it there a few years ago when he had a similar reaction. I made the same mistake back then."

She studied Kat's face. "Tell me. What happened to your parents?"

Kat let out a long sigh. "The picture... That was the last day we saw our parents alive, Ariana. Right before our lives changed forever."

She could see the pain in Kat's eyes, after all this time. "I know losing your parents hurts, and I don't mean to make light of your pain at all, but I have to wonder why Matt has taken this so much harder than you, even to this day?" Ariana wasn't sure how Kat would take the question, but she meant it in the sincerest way possible.

"It's simple, Ariana." Kat stared into her eyes. "He thinks their deaths are his fault."

SEVEN

By the next morning, Ariana had decided. One sleepless night and a gnawing ache in her tummy were the most prevalent indicators for what she should do next.

She needed to head home—and lick her wounds all the way there.

Merry Christmas to me. Bah humbug.

Her bags packed, she parked them by the front door in the inn's entryway. After piling her coat, purse, and camera bag on the bench, she made her way into the kitchen. According to the local news station, the storm had moved out of the valley, heading toward the coast; the main roads and interstates gradually reopening. A quick call to local law enforcement informed her that the county roads were mostly clear between the inn and downtown Dickens, but that she should proceed with caution between Dickens and the main highway.

She could likely make it to Boston easily over the next day or two and then get a flight home. She didn't mind taking her time. Having done a little research online for potential accommodations between here and Logan International, she'd jotted down a couple of hotels and their phone numbers on a Holly Hill Inn note pad and tucked the paper into her purse. She'd make her plans once she was clear of Dickens. She was in no hurry to get to California, really, and could use the hotel time to write and upload her blog posts.

Besides, she wanted to be alone. There was a lot she needed to think though. Even though she'd suffered through a sleepless night thinking, she hadn't come close to coming to any sort of resolution about her feelings for Matt, and why his rejection cut so deep.

What she knew was that she couldn't stay in Dickens any longer.

There was no reason to stay at the inn, and every reason to leave. She had experienced Dickens, taken pictures and recorded story ideas, and had a great stay. Now, it was time to go back home and get to work on next-year's Christmas article pitch to the national magazine.

Besides, she had lost the Christmas spirit—and truthfully, that worried her as much as anything. She might just need a Christmas miracle to get her back on track.

Stepping into the kitchen, Ariana noticed Kat glance her way as she stood flipping pancakes. The kitchen clock over her head on the wall said it was just before seven o'clock. *They all must have slept in. Good.* Aimee bounded off her stool at the kitchen island and rushed toward her. Dylan looked up from his coffee.

"Well, there she is," Kat said. "Coffee?"

"I would love some. Do you have a to-go cup?"

Kat stared. "Oh, no. You're not leaving."

It wasn't a question. It was a rather firm statement of fact.

Approaching her, Ariana said, "Yes, I am. I thought about it last night. I made a mess of things and it's best I go now. I hope you understand."

"But we haven't made the gingerbread houses yet. And tonight is Christmas Eve. You don't want to be alone on Christmas Eve, Ariana."

To be straightforward, she may not have thought her plan through. Tomorrow *was* Christmas. Nevertheless, she'd decided. It would be fine, and she could use the alone time to think. She stepped closer to Kat. "If I can be honest, I don't think I have it in me to be festive and cheery today. I wouldn't be good gingerbread house making company."

"Well, I've never seen a gingerbread house making session where people are all doom and gloom. It might do you some good, Ariana."

She shook her head. "No. It's okay. I have posts to write, and I can do that in the hotel room."

"And you can also write upstairs in the room you've stayed in the for the past two days. Forget the gingerbread. Just stay. If you leave, you'll wake up tomorrow morning alone in a hotel bed on Christmas day. I'll not have that."

Dylan stood up and went to the coffee maker. "It's settled. You're not going anywhere." He poured another cup and then took a sip, looking over his cup at her.

She appreciated their efforts and their words, but her mind was set.

"Thank you both, but I've already made my plans. This is for the best. Besides, the three of you deserve some family time, and I don't want to interfere."

Aimee sidled up beside her and tucked her little hand in Ariana's. "But you are family. I don't want you to go. I have a stocking for you and everything." Small tears formed on Aimee's lower lids.

Crouching down, she searched the child's eyes. "Oh sweetie. That's so nice of you. I would love to share your

Christmas Eve tonight, but I'm just not able to. I need to go home to my own family."

"But we are your family, too. Right?" Aimee looked at her mother.

Ariana followed her gaze. "What?"

Kat let out a breath. "It's something Aimee asked for in her prayers last night. For you to be part of our family."

Aimee nodded. "And it's on my wish list for Santa."

To say she was overwhelmed would be an understatement. Ariana blinked back tears and reached for Aimee, holding her tight. "You are such a sweet girl. I love you to pieces."

"I love you back, Ariana," she said. "Please stay?"

Standing, she swiped at her tears with one hand, and held Aimee's small hand with the other. "Aimee, I can't stay this time, but I do hope I can come back and visit again. Maybe next Christmas?"

The girl teared up more. "Okay. Promise?"

It was all Ariana could do to hold back a sob. "I promise."

"But how do I know?" Aimee looked up at her with expectant eyes.

Ariana bent again and whispered. "Just believe, little one. Just believe." *Am I saying that to Aimee, or to myself?*

Aimee nodded and flashed a toothless grin.

"Now, back to your breakfast."

Aimee climbed onto her barstool, and Ariana turned to Kat. "Can you meet me at the front desk? I still need that signed photography waiver."

She dried her hands on a dishtowel. "Of course. I forgot all about that."

Ariana kissed Aimee on the cheek. "Goodbye. I'll see you again." Then she looked at Dylan. "It was so nice to meet you, Dylan."

"Likewise. Please come back again. I mean that."

"I will."

She headed for the entryway. Once there, she turned to Kat. "I left the waiver on the desk. You can sign and return to me by email when you get a chance. But Kat, there is one thing I want to say before I leave."

"Ariana?"

"I am truly sorry. I meant no harm. I wish... I wish I could rewind the whole scenario and make it better. My heart aches that I hurt Matt. And you. I would never intentionally hurt either of you." She paused, glancing away. Words escaped her.

Kat grasped both her hands. "Ariana, it's okay. I understand."

"Matt doesn't."

"He will."

"I'm not so sure."

"Give him time."

Exhaling a breath she'd held for way too long, Ariana squeezed her hands back. "I wish he had given me a little time, at least. We've barely had time to get to know each other. It was over before it even started, it seemed. I doubt if more time will make it better."

"I'm praying you are wrong, Ariana. Secretly, I wished for you to be a part of our family too."

Her heart jerked a little at Kat's words, her cheeks warming. "I'm not sure I believe in love at first sight, Kat. I'm darned sure Matt doesn't."

Kat dropped Ariana's hands and shrugged. "Our parents did. They married young and quickly, and once they did, never looked back."

"They were special. I can tell. But Kat, Matt and I, we are total opposites in the Christmas department. It would never work. And honestly? I can't have his bah humbugish attitude rubbing off on me right now...or anytime."

Frowning, Kat leaned into the desk. "I understand. But Ariana, if he wanted you to give him another chance, would you?"

Would she? How do I respond to that?

"Oh, Kat...."

"Can I convince to you stick around a little longer? I'm sure he'll come back to the inn sometime today, his tail tucked between his legs."

Turning, she pulled away from Kat and reached for her coat. "No. I need to go. And if Matt wants to find me, I'm sure he can figure out how." Leaning in, she gave Kat a kiss on the cheek. "I can't thank you enough for the beautiful stay and for your hospitality. I'll be sure and send you a link to my blog posts and I assure you they will all be positive."

Kat smiled. "Please do. I look forward to reading them."

Ariana donned her coat, then swung her purse and camera bag over her shoulder. Grasping the handle of her roller bag, she paused, looking at the front door. "Kat, when you see Matt, will you tell him goodbye for me?"

Kat put herself between Ariana and the door, making direct eye contact. "Why don't you say goodbye yourself? I can tell you how to get to his farm."

"You are persistent." She knew what Kat was doing. "No. I'm the last person he wants to see."

"I wouldn't be so sure."

She fished her car keys out of her purse. "I'm sure. He was quite upset. And quite clear." Tears stung her eyes again. "He wouldn't let me explain. I tried to apologize, but he was not hearing anything I said. I feel like things are left undone... But Kat? Now is not the time. I'm not sure my heart can take it."

She turned and twisted the doorknob, not wanting Kat to see the tears streaming down her face.

"I think his heart is broken, too."

She glanced back. "Is that what I'm feeling? A broken heart?"

"That's for you to decide, Ariana."

She sniffed and then nodded.

"Stay around a while and think about it."

Shaking her head, she said, "No. This is not the place for me to wallow in what I did wrong and how I feel. Again, thank you so much."

Moving out the door, she rolled her luggage across the porch and down the brick sidewalk. She was leaving Holly Hill Inn on a much clearer day than when she'd arrived—weatherwise, that is. Her head was anything but clear, however. As she circled the drive and drove away, she watched the red clapboard home fade in her rearview mirror.

What a mess she'd made of things.

MATT PULLED another box off the shelf and set it on the floor in the back room of the hardware store. This one was full of garland. The one before that was filled to the brim with velvety red ribbons and bows. And the one before that held an overabundance of glittery plastic balls in assorted sizes and colors.

His mother would string the garland across the front of the store and hang the larger plastic balls beneath it. The bows were for the front windows. Somewhere in the backroom there were several giant wooden cutouts. If he dug deep enough, he might come across a nativity scene or two that his mother had painted for church displays. Or, he might find the elves, Santa and Mrs. Claus, a big red sleigh and all the reindeer, including Rudolf, that used to circle the town gazebo when he was a kid. His mother had painted so many of these Christmas caricatures over the years, he had no clue where many of them ended up.

She had loved every minute.

Much of her work was featured in various Dickens' Christmas displays throughout the years. She'd been frequently touted as the town artist and creator of the "curious and whimsical Christmas cutouts," as dubbed by one writer, in local and regional magazines and newspapers.

His thoughts immediately shot to Ariana. If she'd been around back then, she'd likely be one of those people with a camera eagerly capturing the quirkiness of his mother's art. Pushing out a sigh, he was suddenly sorry for being silently annoyed with her desire to capture the beauty of the season and the Christmas spirit.

He should apologize.

If his mother were still alive, she would have latched on to Ariana just like Kat and Aimee had. They both loved Christmas and capturing its spirit through their art—his mom with her paints; Ariana with her words and her camera.

Suddenly, his heart grew warm thinking of both Ariana and his mother together in his thoughts. The two of them in his head made him smile, inside and out.

Returning to his task, he pushed aside a couple of old, artificial trees, and spied one of the Christmas characters leaning against the back wall. He brushed away the dust.

"Well, hello Santa. It's good to see you again."

And if Santa were here, the other pieces were likely here too. Good.

He'd been up all night. Hadn't even been to bed. In fact, he didn't go home as he'd told Ariana and Kat he would, but came straight to the hardware store after leaving the inn. Here, in the back room of the hardware—the place that used to be his mom's art studio, and where she had stored years and years of

Christmas paraphernalia—he'd had a come-to-Jesus meeting about Christmas, his parents, and his stubborn Scrooge attitude. It was a serious meeting that included himself, the absent Santa and the missing baby Jesus from the nativity scene, and probably his Maker, about how it was time to get his head on straight about all the above—and about why he'd been avoiding anything to do with the holiday for way too many years.

Oh, he knew why. He kept playing the same tapes over and over in his head every holiday season. And it was time to forgive himself.

Time to stop.

Besides, now he had a good reason—and her name was Ariana. While he couldn't rationalize the reality of loving her so quickly, he knew that love was what he was feeling in his heart. And if his parents could fall in love at first sight, so could he. Right?

But could Ariana?

Did she love him?

Could she *forgive* him?

With every box he pulled off the shelf and rummaged through, he saw Ariana poking through the boxes in the attic at the inn. Her smiling face, full of cheer and happiness, graced his thoughts and poked at his emotions.

She was an unending bundle of joy...and he'd squashed her without a backward glance.

He'd been wrong last night, and he needed to apologize. Wanted to apologize. For so many things.

But first, he had a few urgent tasks to take care of, and then he'd head back to the inn. She was staying through Christmas, so there was time. Hopefully, he could make amends with Ariana and see if they could try, once more, to get off to a better start.

They'd barely had a chance.

But there was one more thing he wanted to locate if he could.

Pushing through the stacks of boxes, he stood back and glanced over the dusty shelves, his gaze spanning the back half of the room. Finally, there, about midway up on a shelf, was the old hat box he'd been looking for. He pulled it down, dust drifting from the shelf. He blew off another layer of grit from the top and set the box on a nearby table. Carefully removing the lid, he then pulled out a handful of old photographs.

He sat on a nearby chair, suddenly exhausted, but determined. One by one, he looked at every picture in the box of Christmases past. Remembrances flew by through tears and even some laughter. He could only hope by facing some of the happy Christmases he'd experienced in the past, could he somehow carve out happier Christmases in the future.

EVEN WITH THE chaos of last evening, Ariana couldn't resist one last visit to downtown Dickens. Her heart was heavy, and maybe another look at Dickens would soften the hurt she felt inside—just a little. After all, she'd come all this way. Right? Even though the situation with Matt was weighing heavily on her, there was something about the town, some sort of magnetic pull, that drew her in.

Perhaps a small bit of Christmas cheer would help.

She parked near the gazebo this time, rather than on the other end of town, like before. Pulling into a parking spot, she glanced about the square and focused on the holly-draped wooden structure off to the side. Town workers had been busy clearing snow from the sidewalks and the gazebo, and she decided that she needed the perspective of looking down Main

Street from the gazebo steps for her blog. She had not taken that angle the other day.

Removing the camera from its case, she changed out the lens and exited her car. She approached the gazebo, climbed the few steps up to the landing, and turned around to look down Main Street. A few people were milling about—last minute, after the snowstorm, Christmas Eve shoppers, she suspected. Taking a deep breath, she inhaled both sights and smells of the day. Fresh coffee was brewing somewhere. The air was crisp. The sky clear. And the day just beginning.

Ariana raised her camera, focused, and took the first picture, aiming straight down the street. She angled herself a little to the right, shifted perspectives slightly, and snapped again. Moving the camera along the street, she focused on a man and woman heading into Leslie's Bakes & More. She snapped another picture. Then past the pastry shop, she panned the camera lens down the street, rounded the corner and grazed over a couple of shops at the end.

Wait. She backed the camera up and looked again, focusing on the shop near the corner. Pointing the lens a little higher on the building, she pulled the camera away from her face and blinked.

"No. It couldn't be."

She brought the camera to her eye again. *Yes, it is.*

Dickens Hardware popped into sight, all decked out for Christmas with Santa, his reindeer, and more.

"Well, I'll be."

A little giddy with excitement, Ariana lowered the camera and examined the hardware store's facade. In the night, Santa had done a little magic on the storefront. Had he also done a little magic on the man who owned the hardware?

She bit her lip. "Should I try to find out?"

Without hesitation, she grasped her camera tighter and

made her way down the freshly swept steps of the gazebo and got into her car. As she started the engine and backed out, she wondered if she was doing the right thing.

If Matt were there, would he want to see her? Would he send her on her way, embarrassing her one more time about her innocent miscue? She didn't know.

But she had to try. Didn't she? One last time?

She pointed the car down the street, rounded the curve, and headed for a parking spot in front of the hardware. After parking, she faced the structure and studied the wooden cutouts propped in front.

She blew out a breath. "Matt Matthews, you broke my heart last night. Hurt me real bad. And on Christmas Eve, no doubt. I don't know what these decorations mean, but I know they weren't here a couple of days ago. Have you changed your tune so quickly?"

Not likely, a voice in her head said.

But there was proof. Right? In the decorations?

Ariana opened her car door and slowly stepped onto the pavement. She stood for a moment, looking at the front door, wondering if Matt would open it and pop his head out any second.

He didn't.

Gently, she closed the car door with a click. She ambled toward the front of the building and took a long moment to stare into the big display window. She couldn't see much. It was dark inside.

"Store's closed."

Ariana jerked to the right. "Matt?"

A man wearing a puffy jacket and a knit hat pulled down over his forehead stopped in front of her and nodded toward the hardware. "Naw. He's gone. He always closes this time of the year. Wish he wouldn't because sometimes you just need stuff, but he does." The man shrugged and continued. "Of course, I guess he has his reasons." He peered directly into Ariana's eyes.

"I suppose so. I thought perhaps...."

"Naw, see? He even has a sign on the door."

"Oh?" Ariana took a few steps closer to the door. She saw a piece of paper taped to the inside of the window:

CLOSED UNTIL THE NEW YEAR

And then she spied the tiny letters beneath and peered closer:

bah humbug

Ariana stepped back, turning to say something to the man, but he was already down the street. She glimpsed him heading into the wine shop about three doors down. Lowering her eyes, she grasped the doorknob on the hardware store door and jiggled it a little.

Locked tighter than a drum.

"Who am I kidding? Matt must have put out the decorations before he left the other day."

Without a backward glance, she got into her car and headed for Boston.

EIGHT

The butterflies inside Matt's gut were an unusual thing for him. He was not the nervous or anxious type. He didn't have bodily or physical reactions to emotional things. But the closer he got to Holly Hill Inn, the more his stomach quivered.

He had to apologize to Ariana, and he had no clue how she would react, or if she would even talk to him. What he knew was that he didn't want another hour to go by before he told her how sorry he was for acting like an ass, and for saying the things he had said.

And on Christmas Eve, of all days.

He'd surely ruined her Christmas. Ironic, huh? That he'd be responsible for ruining the thing she'd come to Dickens and Holly Hill Inn for? To experience the magic of Christmas?

Magic. Bah. He'd killed that.

When would he learn?

Pulling onto the circular driveway to the inn, he braked hard. "I have to get the magic back. Now."

He took a deep breath, exhaled, and stared at the red clapboards framing the inn. "Now or never."

Exiting the truck, he slammed the driver's side door, jogged up to the porch, and grasped the doorknob. As he twisted it, the door jerked open, the knob out of his hands.

"Uncle Matt!"

He grinned. How could one not believe in magic with this beautiful child around? "Hey ya, elf!"

"I told you, Uncle Matt. I'm not an elf."

Inside now, he lifted her up and swung her around in his arms. "You know, you're right. You're not an elf at all. Those points I saw on your ears the other day? I don't think they were just any old common elf points."

Aimee grew wide-eyed as he talked. "They're not?"

He shook his head. "No, they're not. I think..." He leaned closer to her ear and whispered. "I think they were Santa's special helper elf points. That makes you special."

Aimee pulled back and grinned at Matt. "I want to be a reindeer."

Her toothless smile made him laugh. "I love you, Aimee Hall."

Aimee grasped his face in her two hands. "I love you too, Uncle Matt!"

They stood at the entrance to the kitchen now. Matt put Aimee down. He glanced at Kat and Dylan drinking coffee at the kitchen island. He felt giddily happy and scared out of his wits at the same time.

Their faces fell the moment he stepped into the room.

"Where's Ariana?"

Kat glanced at Dylan and sat up straighter in her chair.

"You're about an hour too late, Matt. Sorry."

His happy place was skidding off. "What? She's supposed to be here through Christmas. Where is she?"

"Gone home." Dylan rose, coffee cup in hand, and headed for the coffeemaker. "If you haven't a clue about that, man, you need lessons in women...and perhaps, relationship building."

Matt stepped forward. "I know I was a little harsh last night, but I didn't think she would leave. I've been working through things all night and I need to see her. I don't understand why she left so soon." The butterflies in his gut had left by now, and in their place, suddenly dropped a gnawing, empty ache.

Kat stood beside Dylan. Quietly, she said, "You broke her heart, Matt. She was hell-bent on getting out of here."

"But tomorrow is Christmas!"

"And she wants to spend it alone."

Frustrated, he paced and raked his hands over his head. "But no one should be alone on Christmas."

He stopped pacing and exhaled, looking at Kat.

"You're right," she said. "And we've been telling you that for years, Matt, but you haven't listened. Until now."

"Have I ruined things?"

"For whom? You? For her?"

"For us."

Kat shook her head. "Maybe. I don't know. I guess it depends on what you do next." She paused, looking him over. "The one thing she said was that she didn't need your negative Christmas attitude in her life, so if you expect to get her back, you're going to have to come to some sort of resolve with the past, Matt."

He agreed. "Yes. And I already had that come-to-Santa meeting last night."

"What?"

He waved her off. "Never mind. I'm good in that department. I just need to find her, but I have no clue what to do next."

Dylan piped up. "What do you want to do, man?"

He caught Dylan's gaze. "I want to apologize. I can't lose her." He suddenly felt frantic inside and a little out of control. "I think I'm falling in love with her."

"They go get her. Find her."

"How?"

Kat stepped up to him and grasped his forearm. Reaching into the pocket of her sweatpants, she pulled out a slip of paper. "Here. I found this on the floor next to the nightstand in her room. I think she forgot it, or it slipped out of her things."

Matt glanced at the paper. On it were the names of a couple hotels and some phone numbers. He snatched the paper from his sister and drew her into a big bear hug. "Thank you."

ABOUT AN HOUR OUT OF DICKENS, Ariana pulled into the parking lot of a big box store, just off I-89. She needed a minute just to gather her thoughts and work out the kinks in her shoulders. She'd done a bit of white-knuckle driving between Dickens and the main highway. The interstate was mostly clear in the right lane and was much easier to navigate than the two-lane roads. Still, she hadn't expected the drive to be as hazardous as it was.

"Geez. You're from California, Ariana. Kat was right. What do you know about snow?"

Nothing. Absolutely nothing.

At the other end of the parking lot, someone driving a pickup truck with a plow on the front cleared the snow, having already moved piles of the white stuff in the area where she had parked.

Leaving the car idling, and the heater going, she stared ahead at the store. It was closed, but there were a few cars besides hers—some with people inside, engines running, exhaust puffing. Early riser customers, she guessed. Last minute Christmas shoppers.

The others were empty, engines off, likely vehicles of workers already in the store.

Glancing at the clock on the dash, she realized the time. She'd left Holly Hill Inn around seven o'clock this morning and now the hour was creeping up on nine. Sitting there, she let a moment of peace and quiet waft over her, closing her eyes and breathing deep. Within seconds, tears stung and rolled over her lower lids—the first cry she'd let herself have since Matt got so angry with her—and she didn't stop them from falling.

As she cried, the tension in her neck and shoulders dissipated. She'd been driving with her arms and shoulder muscles taut the entire time—partially because she couldn't relax and partially because of the roads. It felt good to let go, with no one around to see her, hear her, or ask questions.

Lord knew she'd questioned herself enough over the past several hours.

Why she would assume, after knowing Matt and Kat only a few days, that it would be okay to do something as personal as pull that picture out and place it front and center, she didn't know.

But she also didn't know—and no one had told her, everyone had skirted the issue—why there was so much secrecy around their parents' deaths. Maybe it wasn't secrecy as much as an unwillingness to dredge up the past.

And she'd put the past right in front of Matt's face. Stupid.

Swiping at tears with the back of her hand, she pulled her bag closer and rummaged for a tissue. Finding none, she turned to the console where she had tucked a few napkins from a fast-food restaurant a few days ago. There. Success.

After blotting away lingering tears and blowing her nose,

again she poked through the items in her big purse. "What in the world did I do with that note paper?"

Not finding what she was looking for, she sat back in the seat and stared at the store again—which had obviously opened because people were leaving their cars and heading inside.

"Darn it," she murmured. "I must have left that list at the inn."

Well, no matter. *I'll do a quick internet search for hotels on my phone.* But when she picked up her phone, she quickly noticed the battery was nearly nonexistent. Plus, there was a voice message. Why hadn't she heard the phone ring?

Low battery, likely.

"But I charged you last night! Why are you dying?"

This wasn't good. She needed her Wi-Fi, and she needed her phone. She dove back into her bag, searching for her charger and again, coming up empty. Next, she dug deeper into the console between the seats. She had brought her car charger. She knew she had—she had used it on her trip up to Dickens from Boston.

This was getting ridiculous.

Hotspot. She'd purchased a hotspot from her cell phone carrier just for this trip, having been warned of spotty internet service in some of the rural areas she would travel through. She'd not used one prior to this, so she'd almost forgotten she had it. But if memory served correctly, she could charge her phone with the hotspot device plus get the internet, of course.

She emptied her bag on the passenger seat. Out plopped the hotspot device. "There you are." Sighing, she grabbed up the thing and sat back in her seat. She pressed the button to turn it on and waited.

Cord. She needed a cord to charge her phone. Glancing at the seat, she saw none there. She knew she hadn't spotted one in the console. Had it slipped between the seats or under? She was going to have to get out of the car to look underneath the seat.

The hotspot blinked on in her hand. Then off. Then on again. She saw the lit face long enough to see the red line on the battery icon, the power at only two percent. "You're dead, too?" In disbelief, she tossed the device at the pile of paraphernalia on the passenger seat, then sat back in her seat and laid her head against the headrest.

"I can't believe this." Tears stung again. "No. I will not cry over this. This is not a thing to cry over."

I'll figure it out. No phone. No hotel numbers anyway. No internet. And no GPS map app to guide her to Boston. And tomorrow is Christmas.

Not how she had planned spending Christmas Eve and Christmas day. What happened to her sparkly, tinselly, and sugary holiday world?

Ariana exhaled so forcefully her cheeks puffed out, and condensation pillowed up on her windshield. Sitting up taller in her seat, she stared ahead for a few minutes, thinking. Then quickly, she pulled the shifter into drive, accelerated, and pointed the car back toward the interstate.

"Just. Keep. Moving. Forward."

Ariana navigated around the plowing truck and the snow piles and a few cars entering the parking lot as she left. Once she was back on I-89, she breathed a little easier—until less than a half-mile down the highway traffic slowed significantly, and she came to an abrupt stop.

"Now what?"

The state police had blocked the road with their official vehicles, lights flashing, and were turning cars around. She eased up closer, following the line of traffic—basically because she had no choice—until she pulled up next to a trooper.

Stopping, she rolled down her window. "Good morning, officer. What is going on?"

"There is a major accident up ahead, ma'am," he said. "You'll need to turn around and find an alternate route."

"But I'm heading to Boston."

"Not this way. The interstate will be closed for some time. There are fatalities."

Ariana sucked in a breath. "Oh my."

"Can you move along, ma'am?"

"Yes. Of course."

Ariana followed the traffic and turned around, guided by the troopers directing traffic toward the other side of the road. Once she was heading north again, she just drove, not really knowing what to do next. She supposed could stop at the big box store and gather her thoughts. She could go in and buy a charger there, and maybe a map, so she could find another route to Boston.

Or she could head back to Dickens.

And what would she do once she got there? She couldn't go back to the inn. That was out of the question. She was fairly certain there were no other hotels in the area—she'd searched before she'd booked at the inn. So, she really *couldn't* go back to Dickens.

Could she?

On the console, her cell phone buzzed and jumped. Ariana glanced down to see the caller: Holly Hill Inn.

Quickly, she snatched up the phone while watching the face turn black. "Hello?"

But no one answered. The phone was dead.

MATT DROVE AS FAST as his truck and the roads would let him. He'd called all three numbers on the paper Kat had given him and learned that Ariana had not made reservations at any of those hotels—and that they were all full up for the holiday, anyway. All he knew was that she was heading to Boston, so he supposed that's what he would do, too.

He shook his head. Needle in a haystack.

He'd never find her.

Snatching his phone out of his jacket pocket, he drove on and called Kat. She answered within a couple of seconds.

"Matt? Did you find her?"

"No. Not yet."

"I tried to call her just a few minutes ago. No answer."

Matt sighed. "I don't know why she wouldn't pick up a call from you. It's me she's mad at. I can understand why she hasn't returned my call."

"You called her?"

"Yes, and I left a message earlier."

"I hope you were nice."

"Kat. Do you think I'd call and yell at her again? I feel terrible about that. No, I apologized and asked her to reconsider and come back so we could talk."

He heard Kat blow out a long breath. "Well, that's good. Hey Matt, be careful. There was a report of an accident on I-89. A couple of semis tangled with a car or two. I guess the roads are still a little slick down that way."

The second Kat mentioned the accident, his gut seized. "Oh, my God. Ariana."

"Oh no. Matt. Surely she's not involved."

"Try to call her again. If you get through, let me know. I see lights up ahead. I'll let you know what I find out."

He ended the call and tossed the phone onto the passenger seat. Gripping the steering wheel so tight his knuckles hurt, he sped up, heading toward the roadblock, an ache in his stomach the size of New Hampshire.

No. This was not happening again.

SHE'D SAT PARKED in front of the gazebo in Dickens for at least an hour now. Maybe longer. She'd lost track of time. Ariana knew she had to make some sort of move, and soon. She couldn't sit there all day. She had to find a place to stay the night. She needed to get her phone charged so she could actually communicate with people. Glancing about, she wondered if any of the shops around the square carried phone chargers.

Maybe the hardware. Yeah, right.

The hardware was closed. There had to be some other place.

"Just get out of the darned car and go look," she mumbled. "Stuff will not happen with you sitting here."

She'd sat there entirely too long anyway, but at least she felt comfortable here in Dickens. Until she'd arrived back in the friendly town, she's felt nervous and unsure and, well, rather lost. At least in Dickens she felt good. If only she could bring herself to go back to the inn, she might feel even better.

Her gut ached to talk to Matt. She had so much to say. So much to apologize for. She hated the undone feeling that had encompassed her entire body. Maybe she should try to get in touch with Kat. She would know what to do.

"Okay. Move it, Ariana."

She pushed open her car door, grabbing her wallet off the seat, and locked the car. Spanning the landscape around the square, she spied a drug store next to that yummy bakery with the Snickerdoodles she'd visited a couple of days ago. The drug store looked to be her best bet.

She headed that way.

Over the next fifteen minutes, she secured a car charger for the phone and grabbed a scone and coffee from the bakery. She put the phone on the charger in the car and let it charge while she took up residence in the gazebo.

Leaning into the rail, she sipped her coffee and looked down the square to where the hardware store stood. She eyeballed the big Santa figure, the garland dripping with tinsel, the Rudolph flanking Santa's side.

"When in the world did he do all of that?"

The smell of coffee suddenly became stronger. "Took me a while to find old Santa, but once I did, the others weren't far behind. I figured better late than never."

Ariana whirled. "Matt?"

He strolled toward her from the other side of the gazebo, carrying a steaming cup of coffee himself. "Hi, Ariana. Thank God, you're here."

A bit dazed, she shook her head. "What are you doing?"

"I was about to ask you the same question. I thought you'd gone. I've been trying to find you and you've been here all along?"

She shook her head. "No. No. I was headed to Boston, but the interstate was closed and I didn't know what else to do but come here." Pausing, her stomach trembling a little, she eyed him. "I thought you were at the farm."

His gaze drifted off, looking down the street. "Naw. I never made it to the farm. I came into town last night instead. Spent the night at the store."

"And decorating, it looks like."

"Yes. And that."

He shuffled his feet, glancing lower, and then looked back

at her. "I just got back into town when I saw your parked car. I've been out looking for you. Kat told me you were going home."

"That's right. I am. Was."

"But you're here. In Dickens."

She nodded. "I, uh... Came back." She wondered if what she was about to say would sound superficial to him, then figured she'd deal with it if it was. "I'd like to say I came back to see the town one more time, and well...to take some more pictures. I know you think that's weird and commercial or something, but Matt, it's my business. It's how I pay my bills. And frankly, it's my passion. Besides, other people enjoy my writing and my photography."

"But it's not why you came back?" He stepped closer.

"No. Not really."

"It doesn't matter. I'm glad you did. Ariana? I'm a jerk. To be honest, I don't remember everything I said to you last night, and if you could spare me a few minutes, I'd like to explain some things."

Stepping back, Ariana shook her head. "Wait. Matt. What I just said wasn't entirely true. I was halfway to Boston when I got turned around because of an accident and, well, other stuff, and I just headed toward Dickens. I have no clue what my next move is. I didn't even plan to come back. I just sorted of pointed my car in this direction and ended up at the gazebo. I suppose I just wanted to be here."

Matt's expression was a mix of seriousness and relief.

"Ariana. I saw the roadblock too. I feared it was you until I stopped to talk to the trooper. He described the vehicles, so I knew then you weren't involved, but I have to tell you, it scared me to death to think you could have been."

She stared at him. "I guess it's a good thing I pulled over earlier. I took a moment in a parking lot."

"A parking lot?"

She nodded. "Yeah, I needed to... Well, I needed to cry and get my act together. The past twenty-four hours have not been my finest hours."

Matt moved closer and grasped her elbow. "Ariana, I want to apologize."

"No. I'm the one who needs to apologize, Matt. There is a lot I don't understand. And to be honest, you don't owe me any kind of explanation. I'm just some girl who happened along one Christmas—I don't need to get mixed up in your life."

"What if I want you to get mixed up in my life?"

"Do you?"

"I would like to see what happens."

"Oh, Matt. It would never work. You are Scrooge. I'm Miss Christmas. I don't think—"

"What if I kill the Scrooge act?"

She stared at him. "Can you?"

He took a moment before answering—still, his eyes never left hers. "Yes. I can. But there is more. Can we talk? It's just a short walk down to the store. Do you have the time? Can you make the time? I'd like to share a few things with you."

Ariana bit her lip. She had all the time in the world, so why not?

"Matt, I don't know...."

He took one step closer and reached for her hand. "Please?"

NINE

M att unlocked the front door to the hardware store and stepped back to let Ariana go inside first. Blinking as she moved into the building, her eyes worked to adjust to the absence of light inside, then Matt flipped on a switch and overhead lights flickered to life.

"Wow. What a neat old building," she said, looking around and turning to Matt. "Like something you might see in a movie." Her gaze drifted up from aisles of old shelves and drawers, to the exposed wooden beams and rafters above.

He glanced about. "It is rather cool. There are days I'm sure I don't appreciate it enough."

Ariana eyed him, wondering what he meant.

"Follow me." He took her hand and led her through the center aisle.

The heels of her boots made only a soft sound on the worn wooden floor planks as they walked. Still fascinated by the store and its contents, she took in as much as possible as they approached the rear of the store.

Matt opened a door and led them inside another room.

"It's a mess. Sorry about the dust. I hope you don't have allergies."

"I'm fine." She followed him to a table. Matt pulled out two chairs and motioned for her to sit. She did, and he sat in the opposite chair.

For a moment, he just sat there looking at her, then reached for her hands and held them. With a lengthy sigh, he peered directly into her eyes.

"I might need to just talk for a while."

Ariana slowly nodded. "Okay, Matt."

He gave her a little smile. "First. Last night... I said some things, and I didn't mean any of them, but I didn't know how to react, so I reverted to old behaviors."

Pausing, he watched her face.

"I actually have grown to like your glitter and sparkles and Christmassy attitude, Ariana. I never meant to say I didn't. I was hurting and my words came out that way too, I'm sure."

Ariana moved one of her hands over his. "It's okay, Matt. I understand."

"And I don't want you to think I don't appreciate who you are, or what you do. I know your writing and photography are important to you. And you love sharing the joy of Christmas with others. I want you to know that I get that."

She scooted closer to him. "Matt. We all say things when we're scared or hurt that we don't mean. It's okay. I understand. But Matt...?"

"Yes?"

Sighing, she grasped his hands tighter. "I am sorry about the picture. It was wrong of me to assume it was okay to display it. Had I realized, I never would have placed it there."

"I know."

"My heart aches just thinking about the pain I caused."

"My heart aches thinking of you leaving here because of

me. Of you not enjoying Christmas because of me. And of me not getting a chance to make things right."

Ariana felt his worry and hurt. She watched Matt's eyes dart back and forth, then his gaze shifted, looking just off her shoulder.

He motioned to the table. "I want to show you these."

"Pictures?"

"Yes. A box full of them. Mom often stored things she didn't have room for at the house here. This back room was her studio for a lot of years. Sometimes she'd come here on slow days and work on putting the pictures into photo albums or categorizing them. Dad was a camera buff," he looked at her, "like you, I guess. He took a lot of pictures."

Ariana picked up a few and looked through them. "These are Christmas pictures."

"Yes. The entire box. I went through them all last night."

Ariana lowered her hand with the pictures to her lap. "Matt. Will you tell me what happened?"

She waited.

"I was eleven," he began. "Kat had just turned thirteen. It was the day before Christmas Eve, and I rushed home from my friend's house to change my wish list for Santa. All I could do was rave about the new Razor Scooter my friend's uncle had brought him for Christmas. I wouldn't shut up about it."

Stopping for a moment, he searched her eyes.

"So, of course, that was the day of the lighting and everyone was busy. The picture you found? It was taken that day. Dad set up the tripod and the timer on the camera and took it. Years later, my grandmother found the camera and had the film developed and framed the picture. I had the same reaction then when I saw it.

"But it wasn't really about the picture. It was about the damn scooter. Early on Christmas Eve, mom and dad left for the city. They told us they'd be back by early afternoon. When five o'clock came around and they weren't home yet, Kat called our grandparents, who lived a few miles away. They didn't answer, but after a while, they pulled into the drive. That's when we learned both Mom and Dad were killed in a car accident."

"Oh, no, Matt." Leaning closer, Ariana gripped Matt's hands tighter. "I'm so sorry."

He lifted his chin. "Yeah, me too."

"It wasn't your fault."

"I've been told that many times, Ariana. But when I learned they had gone to get that damn scooter, all I could do was blame myself."

Ariana exhaled a breath she'd been holding for too long. "If that's true—if that is why they were going, Matt—they did it because they loved you."

He dropped her hands and stood. "I know. But I sure as hell would have rather had them in my life the past fifteen years, than a scooter that would have lasted until the new wore off."

"That's the adult you talking now, Matt. Not the kid you. Be easy on yourself."

He nodded. "Yes. You're right."

"So, you've been avoiding Christmas ever since?"

"I tolerated it as a kid and through my teens, but the guilt always ate at me. Our grandparents—my dad's parents—did what they could to make things better for Kat and me. Our Mom's parents did too, but they lived in Philadelphia, and we didn't see them as often. Mostly summers. But I could never really shake the guilt, especially during the holidays. As I became an adult, I just avoided it altogether and before I realized it, that guilt became a part of who I am, and made me one sour sucker to get along with during the holidays."

"Did you go to live with your grandparents?"

He shook his head. "No, they moved into the inn. They wanted keep things normal for us. Kat inherited the house eventually, and the inn business. The hardware store came to me on my eighteenth birthday. Grandpa Calvin died a year before that. Grandma Maureen stayed on for a while, then she moved back to her place. We lost her a few years ago, and their small farm became mine."

He stopped talking and focused on her. "I'm sorry, Ariana. I've ruined your perfect Christmas."

"Oh, Matt. No." Reaching for him, she put her arms around his shoulders and hugged him. "Nothing is ruined. And nothing is ever perfect. We just have to believe everything is going to be better from here on out."

He pulled back, peering into her eyes. "Is that all it takes? To believe?"

"I'm sure it also takes time—but believing in the magic of Christmas never hurt anyone. I do believe in that." She paused. "And sometimes, it helps if you don't have to do it alone."

He sucked in a breath. "I have time," he whispered. "I want to believe."

She grinned. "Me, too."

"And to be perfectly honest," he added, "not doing it alone sounds very nice, too."

Ariana whispered, "I like the sound of that."

Matt leaned closer. "Ariana, will you stay a few more days? I feel like there is so much more I want to share with you. So much I want to learn about you. I know I have no right to ask you to stay, but will you consider it?"

Tilting her chin, she peered into his deep brown eyes and tipped her face up to brush a soft kiss across his lips. "Yes, Matt. I want to stay."

❄

Ariana followed Matt back to Holly Hill Inn. On the way, she pressed the button on the side of her cell phone, now fully charged. Immediately, her notifications popped up.

A call from an unknown number.

A call from Holly Hill Inn.

A call from her parents.

She punched the password for her voice mails while observing the road.

You have three messages. The first message was sent at seven-thirty-five a.m. from an unknown caller, lasting forty-two seconds. "Ariana, it's Matt. I know you don't want to talk to me but please listen. Okay? I'm going to take one more shot here and ask you for some time to talk. I know I was ugly last night. I behaved badly and I want to apologize. Hell, I'm sorry, Ariana. You don't deserve what I dished out. I have no excuse. I screwed up and I want to make amends. Please? I'm heading to the inn now. I hope you will find it in your heart to see me when I get there. Please." A silent moment passed but the message didn't end. Then quickly, he added, "Ariana, I'm falling in love with you. Please let me apologize."

Matt was falling in love with her?

Message number two, sent at eight-twenty-nine a.m. from Holly Hill Inn, lasting twenty-one seconds. "Ariana, this is Kat. Please call me when you get this message. I'm worried about you. There is a wreck on the interstate, so the roads aren't so great. If you get this, turn around please, and come back. Besides, Matt was here. He's a mess. And he's trying to find you. Please come back and talk with him."

Message number three, sent at nine-forty-five a.m. from Doris Angelo, lasting eighteen seconds. "Sweetheart, it's Mom. Just checking in. Hope you are having a wonderful Christmas

Eve. We saw the weather on the news, so let us know how you are faring. Call us please? Love you."

End of messages.

She called her mother first, assuring her she was alive and well and safe from the storm. Ariana shared she was indeed having a wonderful time, would send pictures soon of the magical Dickens, and that she would call her again in the morning, on Christmas Day.

Since they were just a few miles from the farm, she wouldn't call Kat back. And Matt? She would see him soon.

Smiling, she tailed his truck, feeling like she was following him into their destiny.

Matt pulled into the circle drive at the inn and parked. Immediately, he pushed open his door and jumped out of the truck, looking back to where Ariana was parking behind him. Her door popped and she rushed forward. He was at her side in seconds.

"Oh, Matt," she breathed. She took one look up at him with her big blue eyes and then wrapped her arms around his neck and hugged him. "I think I'm falling in love with you too."

He cocked a brow. "You got my message?"

"Yes. Finally!"

"Why just now?"

She rolled her eyes. "Long story. Tell you later?"

He grinned and tugged her closer. "I'm hoping we have all night." He paused then, a little panicked by saying that. "Not that I'm expecting... Well, you know what I mean. For you and me to talk and—"

Ariana silenced his bumbling words by putting her lips on his mouth. "Kiss me," she whispered.

He fully embraced her, wrapping his arms around her small, compact body, and pulling her even closer. "Yes, ma'am."

The kiss was exquisite. As their lips pressed together, all tension melted from Matt's body. Her mouth nibbled and teased. Groaning, he clutched the back of her head and came up with a handful of soft, silky hair. Inside his chest, wacky, wonderful things were squeezing his heart.

Letting go and letting himself fall in love her, was so much better than holding onto the guilt and anger.

Ariana deepened the kiss, and he was a complete goner. Breaking away, he whispered, "I think I've already fallen for you, Ariana. My gut ached so when you were gone. I thought I'd lost you."

"I thought you didn't want me."

"I didn't know what I wanted. I was hurt and angry and wrong."

"Matt, I'm so sorry I caused you all the pain."

Stroking her face and peering down into her eyes, he said, "That's all gone now. No more of that. Okay? I love you, Ariana."

Her mouth turned up into a cute, pert grin. Her eyes may even have twinkled. His Ariana was back. "I love you too, Matt."

He leaned in again for another kiss as the front porch door slapped closed.

"They *are* back! Mommy! Daddy! Ariana and Matt are here!" Aimee skipped down the porch steps toward them.

"Where in the world is your coat, elf?" Reluctantly letting go of Ariana, Matt turned to scoop up Aimee.

"Elves don't need coats," she said. "They are used to the cold."

"Well, that's only when they've become acclimated to the North Pole," he told her.

"Accli...what?"

"Never mind."

Kat rushed from the porch and took Aimee. Dylan stayed on the top step, watching, and sipping from his coffee mug.

"Oh, my goodness, child. Come on, let's all get inside." Kat paused and motioned them toward the house. They all moved forward. Kat stared at her brother, then sidled a glance at Ariana. "You're back. Both of you."

Matt nodded. "We are."

"And all is good?"

"All is fine."

Kat blew out a breath that fanned out in puffs on the cold air, stopping at the steps to face them.

Aimee piped up. "Ariana, you did come back. Just like you said. Only quicker."

Matt turned to Ariana and noticed some misty dampness in her eyes.

"I told you I would someday, Aimee."

"I know. But I really didn't think it would happen."

"You didn't?"

Matt touched his niece's cheek. "I didn't either, sweetheart, but this past day I kept telling myself that I had to keep believing it could happen." Glancing to Ariana, he grasped her hand and tucked her into his side. "Sometimes all you need is to believe."

"The magic of Christmas," Ariana added.

Matt cocked his head and looked deep into Ariana's eyes. "My parents married on Christmas day. They believed in the magic, too—but they almost didn't get married."

"What happened?"

"They were on their way to elope when they got caught in a snow squall. They ended up at the Peterson's—remember the names on the sign? The story goes that Elaine Peterson shared some Christmas magic with mom, and she and dad patched things up that night."

Ariana smiled. "There truly is magic at Christmas, isn't there?"

"I believe that now."

"I think it's this place," she told him. "And the people who live here. Holly Hill Inn seems to be a place for Christmas magic...and perhaps a miracle or two."

Matt touched his forehead to Ariana's. "You are my miracle."

She smiled. "You are my magic."

Matt grinned and kissed her lips.

"Come on! Enough kissy stuff. We have presents!"

Matt glanced up to the porch, saw his toothless niece waving frantically, and clasped Ariana's hand. As they walked up the steps, he thought about the turn-around his life had become in such a short time. As he and Ariana stepped up to the front door, he tapped the Holly Hill Inn sign, Ariana's fingers entangled with his.

"Merry Christmas," he whispered. "I love you all."

EPILOGUE

ne year later...

"Okay, everyone. Hold those positions and say cheese!"

Ariana looked one more time through the lens of the camera, made sure all members of her family were in the picture, and checked the timer. Eight seconds.

Racing around the tripod, she took her place at the far end of the group, leaned in, and said, "Smile."

Everyone froze.

The camera finally flashed.

Then, the group broke into a cheer and Ariana rushed back to make sure no one would trip over the tripod. "That's the last one for a while. I promise."

"It better be." Matt leaned in, gazed into her eyes, and kissed her lips. "Here, can you take him? I'm going to help your dad get their gifts out of the car."

"Of course." Ariana took Little Matt out of her husband's

arms. "Can you stash this tripod and camera somewhere safe on your way out?"

"I can."

Little Matt tangled his fingers in her hair.

"Hey, sweetie." She rubbed noses with him.

"Aunt Ariana? Can I hold him now?"

She glanced down at Aimee, and then at the chaotic scene in the sunroom. Cookies were everywhere. Her mom, Doris, was sitting on the sofa chatting with Ariana's sister, Claire. Her sister's two kids were playing with a toy train under the tree. Dylan and Grant, Claire's husband, were watching a football game. Why they all wanted to gather in one room, she didn't know.

"How about you sit by Grandma Doris. I'll hand him to you."

Little Matt was barely two months old, but he was still a chunk and a handful to carry around. Best Aimee was sitting when she held him.

Doris looked up as Aimee plopped beside her. "I get to hold the baby," Aimee told her.

"And Grandma Doris will be right here if Little Matt gets fussy. Okay?" She made eye contact with her mom. "I need to help Kat in the kitchen."

"We're fine here, darling." She waved her off. "Go get dinner on the table."

Standing, Ariana smiled, then headed for the kitchen. Before she left the sunroom, however, she turned back to take in the scene. Even with all the chaos, her heart was full and happy.

Kat snuck up behind her and whispered in her ear. "See, I was right."

Ariana turned. "What?"

She winked. "I told you the first day you got there that you would be here for a long time."

Ariana stepped back and eyed her. "That you did. Who would have thought I would never leave?"

Kat grinned. "I need to get back to the kitchen."

"I'm behind you." Ariana turned to follow her and felt a small hand tuck inside of hers. She looked down. "Aimee? I thought you had the baby?"

"Grandma Doris wanted him."

"Oh, I see."

"Aunt Aimee?"

"Yes?"

"I really did get my Christmas wish, didn't I?"

Puzzled, Ariana crouched down and met Aimee's gaze. "What's that, sweetheart?"

"I got you for my family. And baby Matt, too. And Grandma Doris. And Aunt Claire. And—"

"Whew! Aimee," Ariana interrupted. "Yes, you have all kinds of new family now."

The little girl nodded. "You told me to believe, and I did."

Not being able to contain her tears, she tugged Aimee close and hugged the child. "Oh, honey. I love you so much."

"We both just needed to believe, didn't we, elf?"

Ariana looked up into Matt's eyes. Then standing, she put her arms around her husband's neck and kissed his lips. "And I love you," she whispered. "Believing can be contagious."

"You are contagious..." he said, nibbling at her lips. "Merry Christmas, Mrs. Matthews."

"Merry Christmas to you, Mr. Matthews."

THANK you for reading ***Miracle at Holly Hill Inn***! I love this little opposites attract Christmas story. I hope you did too.

Have you read the first book in the series? Set in 1989, ***Home for Christmas*** tells the story of Matt and Kat's parents, Ben and Jenny Matthews, and their whirlwind, love-at-first-site relationship that almost didn't happen.

I hope you will also consider reading book three in the series, ***The Last Christmas at Holly Hill Inn***. **Preorder** yours today or **scroll on to read more!**

THE LAST CHRISTMAS AT HOLLY HILL INN

Can a couple on the verge of divorce find romance again during their last Christmas holiday at Holly Hill Inn?

Will and Ava Cohen were wildly in love—five years ago. Today, they are ships passing in the night, two professionals driven to reach the pinnacle of their professions. When Will steps in the door of their restored Brownstone in Brooklyn each evening, Ava is already on stage at the Gershwin, playing the role of Glinda in Wicked.

They've decided to call their marriage quits—but not until they spend one more Christmas holiday together with their families at Holly Hill Inn. Traditionally, the family arrives in New York, and they all take the train to Dickens together. Will and Ava plan to share their news on the train ride back home.

That was the plan, anyway. When Kat Hall, owner of Holly Hill Inn, senses something off kilter with Ava and Will, she enlists her sister-in-law Ariana—self-dubbed Queen of

Christmas—to weave some extra-magical Christmas spirit around the couple.

Ava starts looking at her marriage—and Will—differently, and wonders if they've been too hasty in making the decision to divorce. But the train is about to leave the station, and she's unsure if she can halt it—or if she should.

Will this really be the last Christmas they will share at Holly Hill Inn?

ABOUT MADDIE JAMES

Maddie James writes to silence the people in her head—if only they wouldn't all talk at once.

From flirty contemporary romance to darker erotic titles—often mixed with a dash of suspense or a hint of paranormal—James pens stories that frequently blend a variety of romantic sub-genres. The happily-ever-after, of course, is non-negotiable.

Affaire de Coeur says, "James shows a special talent for traditional romance," and *RT Book Reviews* claims, "James deftly combines romance and suspense." Maddie is the award-winning author of over fifty titles of fiction—from short stories to novels—and a Top 100 Bestselling Author. Learn more at http://www.maddiejames.net.

Made in United States
North Haven, CT
26 October 2021

10595123R00073